The building Maria was standing in front of exploded and collapsed to the ground. She tilted her head to better see what was happening when something erupted from the top of the rubble pile.

It was large and sharp and horrible; a dark creature covered with barbed joints. Its armor was a bulky slate gray metal that seemed to absorb light.

Maria shrunk behind a piece of rubble when the skull shaped faceplate turned to look in her direction.

She barely had time to digest the appearance of the monster when something smashed it back down into the rubble.

Shiloh! It was Shiloh!

Maria watched as Shiloh pulled the monster out of the rubble and began pounding it into the ground. But as Shiloh turned the thing around, it sliced him with one of its elbow barbs and blood spattered her face. She tried wiping it off, but blood continued to cover her face. She looked up and Shiloh was disoriented as the monster tore into him.

This was worse than any of her other nightmares.

Maria turned her face from the scene until the sound of a body slamming into the ground beside her forced her to look. It was Shiloh, bloodied and not breathing.

And when the monster turned her way, this time Maria couldn't wake herself.

NOTE: If you purchased this book without a cover, you should be aware that you're missing some really cool artwork and valuable stain resistant features!

This is a work of fiction. All characters and events portrayed in this novel are either products of the author's overactive imagination or are used fictitiously.

THE LAST WITNESS™

BOOK II: THE PROTEAN EXPLOSION

TM & Copyright ©1987-2011, Gerald Welch

ISBN-13: 978-0615509648 (Bookmason)
ISBN-10: 0615509649

Requests for reproduction or interviews should be directed to: marketing@bookmason.com

Official website: http://www.thelastwitness.com

Cover and other artwork by Gerald Welch
Published by BookMason Publishing. http://www.bookmason.com
BookMason is a trademark of BookMason Publishing.

Edited by Donna Courtois: http://www.donnacourtois.com

First printing: June 2009
Second printing July 2011

Printed in the United States of America

THE LAST WITNESS

BOOK TWO

THE PROTEAN EXPLOSION

by Gerald Welch

To Valley
9.13.12

Visit the official website! Join the forums,
Download custom wallpapers and more!

www.thelastwitness.com

AVAILABLE NOW!

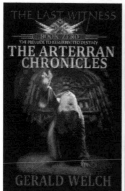
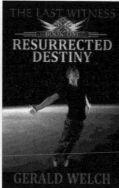

COMING SOON!

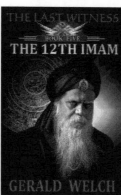
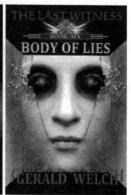

AND FOR A CHANGE OF GENRE:

THE ANDREWS BRIDE by Donna Courtois

When Shelly met Mark, she knew she had found the man she would marry. Now she must convince Mark, her parents and their close-knit community that she has what it takes to be an Army wife. But when tragedy strikes, will she be able to convince herself?

THIS BOOK IS DEDICATED TO:

Frank Peretti, for my first peek into the supernatural;

Tracy Cannon, for remembering the little things;

Howard Price for "a lot";

Ernie Phillips, faithful through all the highs and lows;

and to the word "**borange**".

borange: [**bohr**-inj] - noun

1. A word which has no phonetic English rhyme (i.e., "silver", "liquid", et al.)

The Third Book of
The Last Witness:

Gods of War

Keitz 3:20-21, 25

"I saw the seven angels that stand before God; and behold, one of the angels came before the altar and there was given to it a mighty Sword.

"And the angel filled its sword with the fire of the altar and purified its armour before the Throne Eternal, that it might vanquish the enemies of God.

"Woe to Echad-Erets and all its people, for the rage of Argus is upon them."

PRELUDE

EIGHT YEARS AGO

The cold was excruciating.

Sensations were an ancient experience best forgotten and when the sensation was pain - at any level - it was even less welcome.

But pain was the coin of the physical realm; a necessary evil and Argus, thirD tieR of the unhalloweD, knew evil.

Once a High Angel, Argus was bearer of The Sword; the First Born Exacter of Blood and purpose filled its veins as much as the Holy Fire that filled its Sword. That changed when it chose the voice of the rebel Lucifer over its Creator.

The War in Heaven...

It was the first splinter of chaos in a universe of order. Lucifer led a third of the Angels in a futile attempt to kill man and claim his promise. The war was lost and the thirD were killed. Their bodies were buried in a misty realm and their spirits were forever banished to the physical world of man.

Half of the rebels, including Lucifer, fell to Earth, while Argus and the rest awoke a century later on a world called Ehrets. Similar to Earth, Ehrets was home to the same forms of life, including the children of Adam, but Lucifer and the others were nowhere to be found.

Only a chance spiritual feeler linked Argus to Lucifer again and while Argus had fallen out of trust with the leader of the rebellion, Lucifer knew that it would have to work through Argus if it were going to get anything done on Ehrets.

By separating them, Lucifer explained, their strength had been halved, thwarting a planned second rebellion which directly relied on reclaiming their physical bodies and reuniting as one army. Argus tried every way to escape the bonds of its planet, but access to the supernatural energy that fueled their spiritual bodies ended at the edge of the atmosphere, so it hovered as far as it was allowed, searching the endless realm beyond the skies.

It didn't take long for Argus to detect something alien to the physical plane; a natural violation of space, turned in on itself, between the orbits of the central planets in Ehret's solar system. But unlike common anomalies such as quasars and black holes, this anomaly emanated an identical energy pattern on both the spiritual and physical planes.

Argus noted that the Host used the anomaly to traverse from Ehrets to Earth and that's when it remembered where it had sampled the energy pattern. After they were killed, the demons' bodies were dumped in a realm forever separated from the physical and spiritual; a pocket universe and while it no longer existed in the body that once housed its ethereal being, Argus could still taste the energy that housed its corpse.

The anomaly wasn't just a portal; it was the makeshift graveyard for Argus and the other rebels. Incorruptible to the ravages of time, the carcasses would never decay and if they could reach them, they could easily reanimate their physical forms.

From the moment of that discovery, Argus determined to make the trip. Not just to return to Earth to gather for the rebellion promised to Lucifer, but to restore its physical body and gather power greater than it had ever considered.

Perhaps more power than Lucifer itself...

But there was something unstable about the anomaly. After finding a way to escape Ehrets' atmosphere, Argus sent groups of lesser beings through the anomaly to test its theory. Time and time again, a legion would enter one side, but only a handful would exit. Sometimes, none escaped its maw, but there was never a shortage of volunteers. The promise of increased power and reunion of the body made the trip worth the risk.

The few who survived passage became immortal once they reached Earth and their stories were carved throughout the history of mankind. Known as Zeus and Odin and Fujin and Shiva and Olorun and Shamash, (among others) they described the anomaly as a dimension of white static, hostile to all life that passed through. Only the Host seemed immune to its destructive environment, so Argus conserved power to ensure it would be one of the few who survived the trip.

And when the time finally came, Argus manifested on the physical plane as a shadow, attaching itself to a vessel designed to traverse great distances in space. The plan was simple: maneuver the craft until it was within the anomaly's grasp, then Argus would hide inside the ship. After its body reformed, it would lay waste to every living being inside the vessel and travel safely to the other side.

But things changed.

Argus detected a wave of emotion, familiar but untimely, wash through the crew. Explosions rocked the vessel, as the life pods still docked in their bays were destroyed. Argus didn't know what caused the damage, but it made its job that much easier.

As the ship fought the gravitational pull, Argus manifested on the physical plane as a shadow and violently twisted. The ship immediately accelerated towards the anomaly. In its temporary physical manifestation, Argus could feel the pull of the anomaly even at this distance. The ship's crew would soon feel it, but by then, it would be too late.

As the ship crossed the event horizon, Argus relaxed toward the back of the ship to conserve energy. The journey would be very stressful, even for one of its stature and Argus couldn't risk being caught outside the same way others had been, forever lost within the white hell, as it had come to be known.

Then its awareness was torn from the ship as a presence approached. A Paradox - both spirit and man - the being arrived on the physical plane outside the vessel. Argus, who had never seen or heard of such a being, much less its ability to survive the brutal vacuum of space, instinctively hid in the shadows of the wings.

The Spirit-Man threw himself in front of the ship, slowing its descent. The being was somehow familiar to Argus, but something was blocking its memory. In fact, it noted that many things about this ship were being hidden. Frustrated, Argus slithered to the back of the ship and pushed. The ship regained forward momentum and the hull began to collapse in the hands of the Spirit-Man.

Realizing that a breach was imminent, the Spirit-Man rushed to the port side, grabbing the wing, attempting to use the ship's own momentum against the anomaly to twist the vessel out of its grasp, but metal fatigue had already passed the critical point.

Argus saw its opening and pushed with all of its might. The strain was too much and the outer part of the wing sheared off into the Spirit-Man's hands. The vessel careened violently into the anomaly, but Argus didn't have time to gloat.

The moment of entry was blindingly painful.

Needles of cold sliced through its quasi-physical form and Argus held on by bonding with the ship at a molecular level. As the ship steadied, Argus surveyed the damage. Side panels were buckling, threatening to implode.

It could not allow the ship to disintegrate. Without the ship's protection, it risked becoming just as lost as the lesser beings that were already stranded in the White Hell.

Argus concentrated, calling its physical body to itself. The ethereal nature of its being began to solidify into a corporeal body as it clung to the outside of the ship. Tendon and sinew wrapped around freshly reclaimed bone, but the biting white matter of the anomaly tore the flesh off as soon as it formed. A spark of anger ignited in Argus' chest as it abandoned its five thousand year old plan to reclaim its body and its new power.

Survival came first.

Argus would have to possess someone onboard. There were twelve beings inside; a young boy who was beyond its touch; two females, also beyond its touch; and nine men. As it cataloged their presences, the life forces of three of the men evaporated.

A struggle was occurring inside. Of the six remaining men, four were beyond its touch. Of the other two, one was dying. The last man would be Argus' only hope for survival.

Argus pushed a single word toward the man: HIDE! and followed its command with a wave of dread. The man instantly complied, abandoning his post to seek the safety of the armored weapons bay. He would remain there until Argus repaired the ship. Argus stretched itself around the hull, performing a pseudo-weld of the weakened panels.

The trip through the anomaly was outside normal time, so there was no way to determine how long it would take. Argus had already become numb from exposure, unable to move, much less perform delicate operations. It would have to anchor to the hull for the duration of the trip. It spent its anger in curses, screaming blasphemies as white matter tore through it, slicing off the remainder of its physical body.

"*Surrender!*" it seemed to yell.

Then it was over.

The ship re-entered normal space and the pressure was gone, but the voyage had taken its toll. Argus would soon shut its own body down to repair the damage it had taken.

Argus held on as the ship traveled to Earth.

The craft landed and Argus watched the young boy that was inside the craft walk out toward one of the buildings on this new world as if he belonged there. Waiting for the others to come out, Argus realized that there were no other life forms on the ship. What had happened while it was distracted?

Looking back at the boy standing at the door of this building, Argus tried to read the words in front of the building, but it was written in an unknown tongue. Without access to a human that spoke the tongue, the sign remained foreign scribbles.

The ship started to leave and Argus released its hold, falling invisibly to the ground. In its weakened state, it took too much effort even to stand.

The front door opened and a middle aged woman welcomed the young boy in. Argus tried to follow, but there was something about the building that would not allow it access.

When it looked up, the reason became apparent.

Twelve Guardians stood around the building, and all twelve were watching Argus, swords drawn. Shaking with impotent rage, Argus knew they were of the lower Tiers, though it didn't recognize any of them. If its full strength were available, Argus would crush them, just to defy them and their hold on this world.

A great wave of weakness passed and Argus collapsed to the ground.

When it awoke, things had changed.

Years had passed, though it couldn't tell how many. Guardians were no longer posted around the building. Argus walked inside only to find that it had been abandoned some time earlier, and was now home only to vagrants and wanderers. Another wave of weakness passed over Argus and in its last conscious moment, it surrendered its hold on the physical world and entered one of the men sitting behind some boxes.

Instantly, the man screamed and fell to the floor.

The white hell had been replaced by darkness, but it would one day awaken and, on that day, hell would return.

Argus would create it.

TODAY

The trip home from the graveyard was somber. This was the second time Shiloh Wagner had attended his best friend's funeral. Everyone at the first funeral thought Brad Murray was inside the sealed casket. After his grave was exhumed and found to house a homeless man whose limbs had been removed to mask the weight difference, the FBI had begun an investigation of the funeral home.

Shiloh knew why Brad's body had showed up days later at the exact spot where he had originally died. Brad had died before the first funeral, but just as the last spark of life exited his body, he sold his body and name to an army of demons, resurrecting Brad as a modern day Legion. He then went on a killing spree that was supposed to end with Shiloh's death.

Just a month earlier, Shiloh wouldn't even have been able to wheeze strongly at Legion, but that was before his transformation. Shiloh had been fighting for his life in a hospital when he felt two clicks in the back of his head. He involuntarily grabbed a breath and his lungs filled with air for what seemed the first time in his life. He was healed. More than that, Shiloh inherited the power of Arter - his world's Samson – but barely had time to acclimate himself to this new reality when his friend, possessed by an army of demons, tried to kill him.

Despite his newfound power, Shiloh was being beaten to death until he had, by chance, touched Legion's skin, which allowed him to exorcise the demons from Brad's body. The temporary extension of life was shattered and Brad died, which brought Shiloh to his second funeral.

These things were also known by Shiloh's parents, who had just learned of their adopted son's otherworldly origins. Shiloh's mother refused to attend the funeral of the boy who tried to kill her son, but his father felt obliged to go. He glanced over at Shiloh, who was quietly staring out the window as they headed home.

"You okay?" George Wagner asked his adopted son.

"I guess."

Shiloh's father felt sorry for Brad. Though he had every*thing* this world could provide, he never had a strong family foundation.

"I just wish he would've let me save him," Shiloh finally said.

"Some people don't want to be saved."

"But this just doesn't *feel* right."

"If that's your standard, then you're setting yourself up for a lifetime of disappointment."

"Mattis says that I should rule this world and continue the line of Witnesses here."

"Well, most people, myself included, might not like that idea."

"But what if I could solve our problems on a worldwide level? On my world we don't have hunger or disease."

"You don't have to rule the world to do that. Besides, what happens when a Witness is wrong? If the most powerful man on Earth is the ruler and that man is wrong, who could stop him?"

"So millions of people should starve, suffer disease and war because of your ideology?" Shiloh asked, a noticeable edge entering his voice.

"Now, hold on. There's no need to get angry."

"This isn't your decision," Shiloh snapped.

"Then you're going to have to put me in your gulag first, because I won't support it. You may think you know how things should work out and even if they did during your life, what's to stop your descendants from being dictators? Didn't you say that your grandfather was a tyrant?"

"It always works out in the end."

"That's not good enough. Why not just help the world as it is?"

"Samson tried it your way and failed."

"So how do you think it would happen? Millions of innocent people would die before they'd let you take over their countries. Are you ready to build your empire on their bones?"

Shiloh looked directly into his father's eyes.

"That's the only thing holding me back."

A chill went through George Wagner as they pulled into their driveway and for the first time he saw his son as the alien he truly was.

Though he was a man of average height and weight, the word 'average' had never applied to Andris Laima. In his early fifties, he easily passed for a man in his thirties. Tanned skin, still drawn naturally across his cheekbones, complemented the barrel chest of an Olympic athlete. Only a small trail of gray betrayed his age.

Born in the class of the ultra-elite, the physical world and everything in it had long ago surrendered any appeal to him. But when a near death experience turned his attention toward the world of the spirit, he found a vast universe where he was a pawn - and a small pawn at that. Over the next few years, he ventured beyond what most people considered "spiritual activity" like séances and voodoo, to real power, and more importantly, access to beings greater than him.

He sat alone on the floor in one of the central rooms in his ninety room mansion and began to quietly sing. He repeated the same verse - six words long - his voice rising into the air along with a trail of faintly acrid blue smoke from the large incense burners placed at the edges of the room. Slowly, an image began to form. A pale face, as tall as a man, hovered in the midst of the smoke. No expression of human emotion was betrayed as the being looked around. Its eyes, although already shadowed, appeared an even deeper black.

"*Compeer...*" The image moaned in a voice that filled the chamber.

"My Oracle, I have done as you instructed," Andris said, motioning to the lifeless body of a young woman bound to a crude stone altar.

"As required, I have sacrificed my *'greatest physical possession obtained without wealth'*."

The Oracle's face turned to see the bloodless corpse and smiled. The ethereal composition of its bony face nearly cracked with the strain.

"Your wife was beautiful. It is a pity that she was of the Name."

"I have done as you instructed."

The Oracle turned back to Andris and its smile evaporated.

"A...small price to pay for what you shall receive," it scolded. *"You have sensed a coming shift in power. These last days will bring forth the greatest assaults from both sides."*

"But this is a personal disturbance."

"There is one already here who will upset the present balance of power on this planet. The one coming will upset your personal sphere of power. You will be involved with both."

"The One coming; have we not prepared for His return?"

"The one coming is not known to you. He brings much trouble to your plans. Behold!"

The meditation room faded into a deep black and Andris rose to his knees to stay balanced as the emptiness surrounded him. A small light pricked his attention and swallowed the room.

Andris Laima was no longer in his home.

He felt the numb transition that was common when entering a vision and found he was standing in a wheat field spreading as far as the eye could see. Small details were often important, and in a vision induced at this level, Andris was determined to remember every detail for later study.

Getting his bearings, he could see nothing but a horizon of wheat and the clouds above. There were no birds, which were common symbols in visions, or even any buildings or trees to help orient him as to his location.

The wheat began swaying as a strong wind moved through the field and Andris paid close attention. Wind almost always signified war. As if to confirm his thoughts, dark clouds began gathering above him. As they formed above, large stones pierced the clouds, crashing all around him, but Andris didn't move.

This was, after all, just a vision and nothing in it could harm him.

As the stones continued to pummel the ground, Andris heard something above him; melodic, but as deep as thunder. The sound built until it crescendoed into a shriek of broken glass and a large column of light punched through the clouds, destroying the stones that had fallen, striking the ground in front of Andris.

A man descended from the light, hovering above the wheat. He wore ancient armor covered with angelic glyphs. His helmet was bordered with razor like feathers shooting from the sides of his faceplate.

"An angel?" Andris wondered. No, somehow he could tell that this was a man, but a man wearing angelic armor.

"Is such a thing possible?" As soon as the thought entered his mind, the man sensed Andris' eyes on him.

"Impossible!" Andris thought. This was only a vision... but even though the man wasn't real, their eyes locked and Andris found he could not look away. He panicked as his awareness, his very consciousness was torn from his body and he found himself circling the scene. He saw the

traumatic expression on his own face as his skin blanched gray and began to draw tightly around his skull. The armored man's vindictive gray eyes did not waver from their target.

Everything he had ever been taught told Andris that he was an invulnerable watcher in a vision, nothing more, but Andris felt his soul leaving his body and broke contact.

The vision collapsed into ethereal ribbons and Andris fell to the floor. As he waited for his senses to return, he purposely avoided the Oracle's mocking stare. It was a few minutes before he could speak and even then, the fear that originated with the armored man still shook his bones.

"This...being. From where does he come?"

An uncustomary pause filled the room as the Oracle's jaw contorted in thought, trying to find words that would be allowed.

"Above," it said, smiling.

Andris looked puzzled. 'Up' was traditionally used to describe north, but it didn't feel right.

"The floors above me in this mansion?"

The Oracle smiled. *"Above,"* it repeated.

Andris desperately searched for the key word that would unlock the frustrating puzzle.

"An air attack?" he guessed.

The face frowned disapproval, but replied, *"On a magnitude this world has never before seen."*

"Will he interfere with the USCHI project?"

The Oracle stared a deep hole into Andris. It never commented on the USCHI project regardless what Andris had promised.

"Please...tell me this man's name."

"I am not permitted to speak his name. The clouds of the enemy block my vision, but I perceive that he comes with the spirit of a prophet and the power of a judge."

Andris' face drew into an angry knot. The Oracle could only speak in riddles and half-truths and it angered him, but not as much as prophets did. The references to a judge would be researched later. His time with the Oracle was nearly up.

"From what nation does he come?"

The image again hesitated, as if testing its response.

"The Arterran Empire," it softly replied, carefully watching Andris' expression, but in all his studies, Andris had never heard of an Arterran Empire.

"Where is this nation?"

"Above," the face repeated.

Andris then understood what the Oracle had been saying and the realization caused him to forget his wife.

"I have a perfect sacrifice for our next session," the Oracle said smiling. *"If you are willing to pay the price."*

"Anything," Andris replied. "Anything."

The brooding face leaned into Andris to the point he could smell its fetid breath.

"Prepare a meal only a dead son may eat."

The bony face dissolved into the randomness of the smoke surrounding it, leaving Andris to ponder its cryptic request.

"Call me," Maria Phillips said, closing her cell. She pulled her car around the side door of the school and as if on cue, a skinny kid with bronze colored hair hopped down the stairs and into her car. Maria's after school trips with Shiloh had become a daily ritual against her better judgment.

For the past week, she had taken him out for coffee after school, but not for the reason Shiloh thought. Each one of those days, Maria promised herself she would break ties, but each day, Shiloh would look into her eyes with such joy and hope that she feared to crush it.

She didn't know what was going on; she never had trouble breaking up with a guy before.

"We aren't even dating!" she argued with herself.

Last week she had begun having nightmares so severe that she feared going to sleep. Something had to give and that something was Shiloh. Besides, the longer she put it off, the harder it would be for him.

Shiloh opened the door for her and walked into the coffee shop with a newly found confidence that she admired. A month ago, Shiloh Wagner had been too shy to even speak to her and his breathing problems were so severe that he could barely maintain a quick walking pace. It was so bad that he missed most of seventh and eighth grade to various sicknesses. But after he was in a near fatal wreck with her cousin Brad, Shiloh recovered; better than he was before the wreck. In fact, he showed none of his earlier signs of sickness.

"He's strong enough to move on," she reasoned.

"I should try out for the football team," Shiloh said with a smile as he brought their mugs to the table. Maria stifled a laugh as he sat across the table from her.

"Football? Tony and Derek would eat you alive."

"Well, I feel good enough to play."

"That's good, but Shay...we need to talk."

Shiloh took a too-long sip from his coffee as his eyebrows arched into a frown.

"Look, we've had fun hanging out the past few weeks, but you're better now and... it's time for me to move on."

Sensing his despair, Maria leaned forward to look into his eyes.

"Hey, it's not like we won't see each other. I just don't want to give you any false ideas. You'll find someone one day. In fact, I know a girl who likes you a lot."

She could tell that her words were dissolving together, their meaning not fully understood. Shiloh dropped his face a bit, reminding Maria of the sick kid she had always known. *Is he going to cry?* she wondered.

Suddenly, someone slapped Shiloh's shoulder.

"Hey Skip!" came a familiar taunt. "Whatcha doin' with my girl?"

Tony Adams sat next to Maria and planted a big kiss on her for Shiloh's benefit. Tony was a defensive linebacker for the school football team; in fact, he was *the* defensive linebacker. Standing a bit over six foot four and weighing two hundred and sixty pounds, Tony was one of the biggest guys in school.

"We're just talking," Maria said.

"Aw, c'mon Skip! Can't get your own girlfriend?"

Shiloh didn't answer.

"Now he's mad. Don't go all Columbine on me, Skip."

"My name is Shiloh."

"Everyone I know calls you Skip, so that means your

name is Skip. What was it last year...Skeleton?"

"I've outgrown that," Shiloh said defensively.

"Ooh, so now instead of being a nerd, you're a geek?"

Tony leaned across the table to return Shiloh's stare and planted a quick kiss on Shiloh's cheek. Tony sat back in his seat laughing.

"There, now you can tell all your little geeky friends you had your first kiss." Tony's playful grin turned into a scowl. "Things are gonna be different now that you can't hide behind Brad."

"That's not funny! Brad was my cousin!" Maria said, and tried to stand, but Tony pushed her back down. Maria shot a look of pure anger at him and Shiloh fumed.

"Let me go, Tony, I'm not kidding."

"Ah, I didn't mean anything. Just letting Skip know how things are gonna be."

Shiloh glared at Tony as Maria sat back in her seat.

"I'm not afraid of you," Shiloh said.

"Skip, you'll be afraid of me long after I blow this town. Heck, your grandkids'll be afraid of me."

Shiloh leaned forward and placed his arm on the table.

"Care to arm wrestle?"

From the look on Tony's face, Shiloh might as well have asked him a math question.

"You want me to break your arm so you can bleed more sympathy outta my girl? I mean, that's what you do, right?"

"No sympathy."

"You lookin' for a lawsuit?"

"No lawsuits from me. How about you?" Shiloh asked. "No lawsuits from you, Tony?"

Tony snorted.

"Shiloh, you don't have to do this!" Maria pleaded. "This won't prove anything."

"It'll prove that I'm tired of being picked on."

"No lawsuits from me, Skip." Tony winked at Maria and placed his arm on the table. His hand almost engulfed Shiloh's.

"Tell you what, I'll give you first go Skip, just to be nice," Tony said, blowing a kiss at Shiloh.

Tony's hand hit the table so fast he didn't even feel it move. He did, however, feel it hit.

And it hit hard.

"Owww, you little prick!"

Tony shook the fingers in his hand to get the feeling back and returned his arm to the table. He looked at his hand with confusion and then back at Shiloh.

"Let's see you try that when I'm ready!"

Shiloh grabbed his hand.

"You go first," Shiloh goaded. "I can be nice too,"

Maria turned her head away and took a long sip from her coffee. The testosterone from both sides was making it hard for her to think straight. If Shiloh was stupid enough to strut against a guy twice his size, he was on his own.

Tony tightened his grip to make it hurt, but Shiloh's expression didn't change. Tony gripped harder, but a confident grin remained on Shiloh's face. Tony twisted his fingers around Shiloh's smaller hand and squeezed with enough pressure to break bones, but nothing changed.

"Are you going to go, or do you just like holding hands?" Shiloh taunted.

That was it.

Tony wasn't going to take any more from this nobody, no matter how much trouble he got in with Maria. He was going to wipe that stupid grin off that stupid face and when he was on the floor crying about a broken arm, he'd remind Maria that he asked for it. The idiot said he wouldn't sue for broken bones, so Tony was going to break as many as he could.

Tony grabbed Shiloh's hand with every ounce of strength he had and slammed Shiloh's arm to the table as hard as he could.

At least, that was the plan.

In reality, Tony pressed until he grunted, but neither arm budged. Tony looked into Shiloh's eyes and didn't see even a hint of strain.

Nothing.

"My turn," Shiloh said calmly and his eyes narrowed. Tony suddenly felt incredibly small. Something inside told him to let go and run away as far as he could. He panicked, trying to free his hand, but Shiloh kept a steely grip and he couldn't move.

"No, man!" Tony said, subliminally recognizing the situation.

Shiloh gripped his hand hard enough to cause tears to burst from his eyes for the first time since he had seen Bambi's mother die when he was six. Tony instinctively locked his wrist as Shiloh slammed his hand to the table and it shattered in three places. The pain rushed up Tony's arm and his anger raged to the surface.

Tony's immediate reaction was to jump across the table and grab Shiloh's skinny neck between his thick meaty fingers and choke the life out of him. He was so mad he actually saw himself choking Shiloh in his mind's eye, but then something larger and more rational than his rage held him back and Tony fell back in his seat.

"Don't bother me again," Shiloh said, standing to leave.

Shiloh turned back, softening the harsh look on his face to look at Maria, who was nursing Tony's wrist and looking strangely at Shiloh.

"I really did have fun," Shiloh said to her quietly and walked away.

He ignored the cussing fit erupting behind him.

Kristi Thomas was happy. She couldn't remember the last time she had felt this good. Ironically, the day couldn't have started off worse. Kristi had to walk to school in the rain. Normally her mom took her, but she was called in to work early. Several kids drove by Kristi, laughing at her little umbrella. A few of her friends honked and waved, but didn't think of stopping and picking her up, so she arrived at school only slightly more drenched than she had hoped.

But the day instantly changed once she got to art class. Kristi sat down next to Shiloh, who was trying to fix his tree sketch. It was a good thing that she didn't like him for his artistic ability.

"Where's Mrs. Curnow?" Kristi asked.

Shiloh picked up the rubber eraser and scrubbed off a few hastily scribbled branches.

"She had to go to the office."

Shiloh had yet to look her in the eye. Kristi brought out her drawing pad and began touching up an obviously finished piece. Shiloh looked over at her drawing and shook his head.

"I still don't know why you even take this class."

"I learn a lot here," Kristi said. "You can, too. Look at your tree. You're trying too hard. Just draw a tree."

"That's easy for you to say."

"Not as easy as you might think. I spent over an hour on this," Kristi explained. "How long have you been working on yours?"

"Uh, I started when I got to class," Shiloh admitted.

Kristi laughed.

"So have you been feeling better since the wreck?" she asked.

"I feel great."

"Good enough to see a movie this weekend?"

Kristi just spit the words out and let the question hang there. What was she thinking? She got ahead of herself. She shouldn't have asked. Shiloh was finishing the last branch and it was taking forever for him to answer.

"Sure," he finally said. "What do you wanna see?"

The question was interrupted as Mrs. Curnow entered the room.

"Sorry, you know how long Principal McCarthy can talk," she said with a wink. "Now, let's see those trees!"

Kristi was angry at the intrusion, but class went by quickly. They were separated into groups and instructed to design a poster for a commercial project. Shiloh's team designed a poster for a new video game of some kind while her team designed a logo for a new perfume. After class, Kristi quickly scurried to Shiloh.

"I can't believe I got a B!" Shiloh said, smiling.

"I can't either," Kristi said, looking at her own B. "So, what movie should we see?"

"Call me later and let me know what's at the theater. Anything but Trek Wars," Shiloh said, making a sick face.

"Deal!" Kristi said, finally smiling as Shiloh hurried to English class.

Luckily, the rain stopped before school was over, so Kristi was able to walk home dry. She bounced to her bedroom, set her bag on her bed and tapped the blinking light on the answering machine.

"Hey K," Maria Phillip's jubilant voice said.

That's odd, Kristi thought. Why would Maria be calling her? And 'K'? Maria was never this friendly.

"Tony and I are going to the *Bandana* Saturday and we wanted to invite you and Shiloh to come with us. What do you think? Call me."

Kristi stared at the answering machine. She had learned her lesson last time. She knew Shiloh had a huge crush on Maria. There was no way she was going on a double date with her again.

Kristi dialed Maria's number.

"You know me," Maria's recorded voice greeted. "And I know you... will leave a message!" A sci-fi blip followed her voice.

"Hey 'M', this is 'K'. Shiloh and I already have plans for this weekend, so no thank you," she said and hung up.

Kristi walked over to her easel, but wasn't in the mood to paint anymore, so she grabbed her clay and began pounding it. As the clay warmed, she began kneading and twisting, flattening some areas, pulling others. She didn't know what it was going to be, but an hour quickly passed before her mother called for supper.

"Be right there!" Kristi called back.

She stepped back, taking a look at her work. It was rough, but she looked at the beginnings of a man's face. The cheeks were strong and the eyes, though forceful, carried a bit of sadness. She could tell then it was going to be one of her better pieces.

Kristi placed a damp towel on it and set it on her shelf of working sculptures to finish later.

"Glad you finally made it to our facilities, General Hampton," Terry Cooper said, waiving the general through a large security checkpoint. "Welcome to what I call Area 52. Pardon the extra security; it's worth it."

General Alan "Hammer" Hampton had a lifetime of experience with security, but even he was impressed. When he first arrived at the small, unassuming plant, he made a mental note to question Stonewell's security when he returned. But after passing through the cheaply painted doors, he went through more checkpoints and armored doors than the Pentagon, only to stop when they reached a chamber with what appeared to be a large black statue.

Standing over seven feet tall, the model appeared to be carved from immense chunks of deeply burnished obsidian. The deeply polished metal of the armor sharply reflected the images of the two men who stood before it.

"This battle suit's bigger than the prototype," General Hampton said. "Hmmph. It's shiny...how much more will that cost?"

Terry Cooper was Stonewell Industries' top salesman and he wasn't intimidated by the general's bluster. The presentation was a formality the general insisted on to cover the hundred thousand dollar 'gift' he received during the demonstration in Thailand.

"Actually, there were four prototypes," Terry reminded him. "We even included the burnished finish that, along with a small electrical current provides stealth like technology in cluttered environments. But this is the only actual production model. We put in all of the bells and whistles from each of the four prototypes."

"I saw the reports. I'm still worried about the power supply."

Terry tilted his head in confusion. The geezer was going to make it look hard. Was someone listening in? No, the sensors at the main gate would have detected any bugs.

"We're working on it," Terry lied.

"It won't do any good if we have to charge it every ten minutes."

"Like I said, we're working on it and remember; no other army has anything like this."

"Cooper, let me make this clear: I don't like you. We've cut some pretty big corners on this battle suit the past two years. I'm retiring next year and I don't want my successor to have to clean up any messes. We need to get this suit up to military specs."

"*Specifications don't exist for something this new, you idiot,*" Terry thought. Putting aside the casual nature he entered with, Terry went into sales mode. As long as he ended up with a signed contract, he would not only put up with the general's last minute guilt, he would beat him at his own game.

"Stonewell is all about business, general. The only messes your successor will have to deal with are the ones this suit leaves on the battlefield. Our second prototype is under development for the more nimble Black Dragon series. It has a reduced energy consumption of over thirty-five percent," Terry again lied.

"It makes you stronger, right?"

Unbelievable. If he was going to try to fake a realistic presentation, he should have at least remembered the one demonstration he actually attended out of the eight he had collected travel expenses for.

"Strength augmentation is old news. As you saw at the demonstrations in Barbados and Thailand, the real advance is in the armor alloy. Each of the prototypes have a base plate of prefamulated amulite surmounted by a malleable logarithmic casing. The production model also has a poly-uranium coating that..."

"Uranium? It's radioactive?" the general said, stepping back.

"Depleted uranium. Look, you haven't got anything to worry about, see?"

Terry unbuttoned the top of his shirt to fish through a small forest of hair and produced a large oval shaped necklace.

"This medallion is made of the same material. It's lighter than aluminum, but over a dozen times the virtual density of a normal sample of depleted uranium. This alloy, general, is the hardest substance known on planet Earth."

He unclasped the medallion from its chain. The general tossed it to gauge its weight, but it was lighter than he had expected and it bounced out of his hand. The medallion made a bright clinking sound like silver when it hit the floor.

The general picked up the medallion and looked at it closely. The alloy was deeply burnished silver and as it turned in his hand, light seemed to disappear into its round, shiny crevices. The medallion was deceptively light, far lighter than any piece of metal this size should be, much less depleted uranium.

"Hmmm. It is light."

"And it's not dangerous. I've been wearing it for a year now and haven't had any problems. Just had a physical last month."

"Depleted uranium's one of the heaviest metals around.

How did you make it so light?"

"Sorry, General; trade secret." Terry said, leaning in like a car salesman about to reveal an insider secret. "Let's just say that we found a way to reconfigure the molecular structure of uranium. Rest assured, our boys will be protected in this baby."

"How many do you have in production?"

"Just the one. Well, until you sign the contract, then we can roll out two more suits the first year, maybe a dozen by the third year."

The general handed the medallion back and turned to the armor.

"You're getting ahead of yourself. Let's see it work."

"Let's do it. Herrington, mount."

Terry motioned to a young man standing at attention against the far wall. The soldier was wearing what appeared to be a modified diving suit. Metallic buttons covered the suit at critical points. His face was exposed, as were his fingers and toes.

With the input of a code, the chest plate opened and the man stepped into the armor feet first. Placing his arms into the arm sockets, and resting his head back into the helmet, the faceplate automatically shut. The chest plate closed and a soft gush of air exited the suit as it sealed.

The entire process took less than forty seconds. The generator whined as it sent energy to the suit and it gave a mechanical belch as it powered up. Several metal plates locked in place, making the battle suit fully operational.

General Hampton stepped in front of the suit, but couldn't see past the dark lenses of the skull-shaped faceplate. A small hum emitted from the armor. The suit jerked and then stepped forward. The general stood his ground, despite wanting to step back. He noticed that the suit was still plugged into the generator.

"*Thumper online*," the suit said.

Not the man; the suit.

"Ah...that's our nickname," Terry said.

"Never liked Bambi," the general grumbled. "Hmmm. Why is it still connected to the generator?"

"We don't unplug him until the last moment. The boot-up sequence is the single largest expenditure of energy. Booting from the generator will give you a good twenty or twenty-five percent increase in battery life."

"Let's get going."

"Herrington, assemble on the range."

Several of the suit's mechanisms began whirring, but there was no other sign of movement.

"The range, Herrington...now!"

No reply. Terry leaned toward the suit.

"Get your tail on the range," he whispered, his eyes blazing.

"What's wrong?" General Hampton asked.

"Nothing. He's recalibrating the unilateral phase detr...acck!"

Terry gurgled as the suit came to life behind him, grabbing him by the neck between its powerful pincers. With a quick whir of metal and gear, Terry's head snapped from his body, shooting forward and rolling until it came to rest near the general's feet. His body stood upright for several seconds as if waiting for the head to stop, then slowly collapsed.

General Hampton took command, but stepped back from the growing pool of blood.

"Stand down, soldier!" he barked.

The helmet turned to face him. The general began to step toward the door, but never had a chance. The pincers tilted down to reveal a small barrel, quickly followed by an enhanced mortar bullet. The general's body was pulverized by the shell and then scattered by the following explosion.

Turning from the grisly scene, the man in the suit yanked the plug out of the generator and burst through the reinforced door into the next room.

Grabbing two small cases marked *'Black Dragon',* he ran to the testing grounds, ignoring the alarms that were triggered as he crashed through each gate. When he reached open sky, he fired his rocket pack, leaping into the daytime sky, leaving behind dozens of soldiers. He didn't even feel the small arms fire that pinged harmlessly off his armor.

"What do you think?" George Wagner asked his assembled family over the dinner table. He rubbed the scruffy hairs on his chin. "I think I'll grow a beard this year. I always thought that a beard gives a man a look of authority."

"Looks can be deceiving," Lillian Wagner, his wife of twenty years replied.

He turned to his daughters. "What do you girls think?"

Julie and Tina stared at each other, not knowing what to say.

"It's scratchy. I don't like it," Tina said, sticking out her tongue.

"If you like it, that's good enough for me," Julie said adeptly.

"Shiloh?"

Shiloh looked up, his mouth full of gumbo. He took a moment to chew on both the food and what he was going to say.

"It's...different."

"How do you know your biological father didn't wear a beard?" George asked with a wink.

Shiloh grabbed another bite and hid his face.

"So, what else is new?" Lillian asked.

Tina held her hand up high. "I saw an angel!" she squealed. "He was on TV. He didn't have wings, but he had a big white cape and helped kids."

Shiloh took another bite and cast a side glance at his parents.

"He's not real," Julie said. "People can't fly."

"He's not people! He's angels!" Tina argued. "Mom, tell her!"

"Well, they are reporting it as a real story."

Julie snorted. Her science teacher was talking about the story earlier in the day and even he was excitedly reading the story to his class. Since he was a child of the sixties Julie and her friends gave him a pass, but she wasn't going to put up with it at home, too.

"Don't tell me you believe this garbage."

"It's not garbage to the mother of the children he saved," Lillian said. "She wants to thank him. And I think he should meet her."

Shiloh had been trying to stay out of the conversation, but his mom's suggestion piqued his curiosity.

"Why?" he asked.

"Someone with that kind of power needs to be reminded why he's doing what he's doing to keep him grounded."

"What?" Julie asked in disbelief. "Dad, is she serious?"

"I don't think he's an angel, but I think it's cool," Shiloh said. "What's wrong with him, Jules?"

"Think about it, Shay. Let's say you get a guy who can really fly, what's next? Aliens?"

George almost spit his gumbo out.

"But what do you do if he is real, Julie?" Lillian asked.

"Then I get a gun, because if there's one, there have to be others and they can't all be good. What's wrong with you guys? I can't believe I'm the only one who thinks this is a PR stunt."

"He's a angel!" Tina yelled. "The TV lady said so! He's not a PR!"

Julie hung her head. Her whole family had gone insane. At least Tina had an excuse because of her age.

"Look, I don't know why, but I got a bad vibe on this,"

Julie said. "I don't want to talk about it."

"Fair enough," George said.

Shiloh quickly scooped the last of his gumbo from the bowl and took it to the sink.

"I'm not feeling well. I'll be in my room."

Shiloh left. George and Lillian glanced at each other; George gave his wife a slight nod. Lillian excused herself from the table and went to Shiloh's room. He wasn't on his computer as she had expected. He was lying on his bed staring at the ceiling.

"Shay, are you alright?"

"Why does everyone think I'll go bad?"

"It's human nature, honey. We don't see news unless something bad happens, so when we see something good, we wonder when the other shoe is going to drop. And that's something you'll need to remember, because when you're out there, people like Julie are going to be watching everything you do. It's hard to get people's trust, and once you get it, you're going to have to be very careful not to lose it."

"I don't think Dad trusts me. On the way back from Brad's funeral, I told him that on my world we only had one leader and it worked there."

"I heard you said it a bit more forcefully than that. He said that you two got in an argument. That's not like you. It's why I suggested you go see that woman in Chicago."

"I still don't understand why."

"You need to see the results of your actions with your own eyes...at least once."

"Well, Mattis can find out where she lives. It just feels weird going to someone's house so they can thank me."

"You need the humility, believe me. Besides, if you saved Julie and Tina from a gunman, I'd want to thank you. Just remember to be gracious. I don't want her to think that you have bad parents."

Shiloh smiled.

"Wouldn't want her to think that," he said.

His mom caught a quick glimpse of Shiloh's smile as he pulled his helmet from the closet, so she turned to leave.

"Mom?" Shiloh called after her. "Thanks."

"Make us proud," she said, closing the door behind her.

Lisa Curtis stood by the side of her bed, silently watching her girls as they slept. They had been sleeping in her bed since the carjacking and Lisa found that she needed their presence just as much as they needed hers. She hadn't thought about it much, but her bed – a California King that her late husband Tom just had to have – was too large for them while he was alive and it was far too large now that he wasn't here.

But it was just right for the three of them.

She left the bedroom to finish some paperwork before going to sleep. Her doctor had prevented her from going to work while she was recovering from her gunshot wounds leaving a ton of work waiting for her when she returned.

She turned the lights on in her late husband's den. It was still laid out like Tom used it, and though it wasn't efficient for getting work done, she couldn't force herself to rearrange anything. It was only fitting, as she was selected to fill his city council seat after his untimely heart attack at thirty-seven. Sometimes Lisa would catch his scent and the tears would begin anew.

What would Tom think? Lisa had been shot and her car stolen while their girls were still in the backseat. After she was shoved out of her car and shot, Lisa tried to chase on foot, but quickly lost strength. She even pushed away the EMT's who were trying to load her on a stretcher. But before she collapsed, in a moment of desperation amidst the cold realization that they were gone, Lisa uttered a prayer for her babies.

Had her prayer made the difference? Would they have

been saved if she hadn't prayed? She couldn't even think about it...

And what would Tom think of a flying man? Lisa didn't know what to think of it herself. She wouldn't even have believed it if she hadn't seen a videotape of the incident herself. A visit to the police station for a lineup confirmed that the man who kidnapped her children was nursing the largest hand cast she had ever seen.

As a student of the law, she believed in the justice system, though another part of her took pleasure in the fact that the man's crime had been punished by a force outside the judicially sterile world of the legal system.

A Higher Force.

"What brought that on?" Lisa wondered. She had never approved of vigilantes and she wasn't going to start now.

"But he's not a vigilante," she argued with herself. *"He's..."*

Lisa jumped as a rap came at the window. There was no fire escape outside her window, just an eighteen story drop. Lisa ignored the sound, thinking she had imagined it until it repeated: the casual rap of someone knocking on a front door.

Lisa reached into her husband's desk and pulled out his pistol. It wasn't loaded, but whatever was outside didn't know that.

Shiloh hovered outside Lisa's window, waiting for a response.

"Why did Mom want me to come here?" he asked Mattis, the artificial super-intelligence housed in his helmet. "Am I just supposed to let her thank me so I can fly off into the sunset?"

"What do you want to accomplish?" Mattis asked.

Shiloh thought about it. He wanted to look into her eyes

and know that he had done the right thing. Shiloh had seen Lisa's story after her daughters were rescued. One cable news story described how badly Shiloh had crushed the carjacker's hand. The reporter said the man's hand would never function normally again and that he planned to file a lawsuit as soon as he could figure out who to sue.

Shiloh didn't feel any pity for the man, but he was worried about his recent outbursts of anger. He remembered being angry at the man for endangering the little girls. Even after he crashed Lisa's car, the man shot at Shiloh and that's when he really got mad. Shiloh grabbed the gun while it was still in the carjacker's hand. He could feel the soft flesh of the man's hand tighten and felt each bone as it began to bend beneath the pressure of his grip but even then, the man was still trying to pull the trigger, so Shiloh squeezed harder. Everything just mashed together; bone and metal, until the gun became a part of the man's hand.

Taken with his earlier outburst at the cafe and his argument with his dad made Shiloh wonder where this anger was coming from.

He had never had a temper before.

Lisa peeked around the corner but could only see a large shadow hovering outside her window. She couldn't see through the curtains from where she stood, but after everything that had happened, she wasn't going to take any chances.

Lisa tore the curtain back - a bit too hard - and the curtain rod came crashing down. Lisa stepped forward and found herself aiming her empty pistol at the man who had saved her children.

Shiloh was hovering outside, lost in thought, when the curtain in front of him pulled open to reveal a woman pointing a gun at him. Though he was expecting someone to come to the window, the sudden movement and sight of the gun caused him to lose concentration and he began to plunge. He regained his composure a few stories below and cautiously floated back up to the window.

By that time, Lisa had opened the large dual paneled windows, keeping the pistol aimed at him. He was shorter than she had imagined, but she recognized the helmet and cape and the cheap black clothing.

"Hey," Shiloh said, raising both hands defensively. "You said you wanted to see me. But I'll go if you want."

Shiloh noted that his voice sounded different. It sounded more... mature.

"Keeping with your desire for secrecy, I have modulated your vocal output," Mattis explained. Shiloh was about to ask Mattis how, but then realized it didn't matter. He probably wouldn't have understood it even if Mattis explained it to him.

Shiloh hovered in front of her window silhouetted by the moon and Lisa let the moment sink in.

He was here and he was real.

Lisa dropped the unloaded pistol on her husband's desk and motioned for Shiloh to enter. She turned the lights on and sat in the chair across from the desk. Shiloh entered the window and stood in front of her.

There was an awkward moment of silence until Lisa extended her hand.

"I'm Lisa, Lisa Curtis; you saved my girls. Thank you for coming."

"How are they doing?" Shiloh asked, shaking her hand. "Your daughters, I mean."

"They're fine...thanks to you, they're fine."

Shiloh stood silently, not knowing what to say.

"Oh, I almost forgot," Lisa said, rummaging through

her purse. She pulled an envelope out. It was thick and obviously filled with money. She laid the envelope in front of Shiloh, who blushed.

"Uh, that's not why I came," he said, handing the envelope back.

"So why did you come?"

"You wouldn't believe me if I told you."

Lisa looked at Shiloh. Close up and in good lighting she was amazed at the contrast between the high quality of the helmet and cape and the black clothing that made it all look like a poor Halloween costume.

"At any given time there are dozens of violent crimes in Chicago. Why did you choose to save my kids?"

"It's my job."

"*But was it a coincidence?*" Lisa asked herself, or had her prayer guided this man to her girls?

"Lots of people have that job, but I don't know any who can fly."

"I'm... different. How are you doing?"

Lisa lifted her arm and Shiloh saw the thick bandages covering her left shoulder down to her elbow. She winced in pain as she lowered her arm.

"I'll be fine," Lisa said. "So, what's your name?"

"I'd rather not say. Just think of me as a witness."

"Do I call you 'Witness'?"

"Actually, I hadn't thought about it. 'Windy City Angel' doesn't quite fit," he said, motioning to the paper next to Lisa.

Another moment of awkward silence permeated the room when Lisa lowered her head and asked her question.

"Do you talk to God, Witness?"

"You mean pray? Sure...well, not as much as I should."

"You answered the first prayer I made since losing my husband. I don't know what I would have done if I'd lost my babies."

Lisa's eyes welled up. She wiped the tears away and motioned to the chair. "Forgive me. Please, have a seat."

Shiloh sat in her husband's chair. Though his opaque visor prevented Lisa from seeing most of his face, she could sense his hesitation.

"This is all new to me, too," Shiloh admitted. "I'm supposed to be a sign of hope. Saving your kids was the first thing I've really done as Witness. Well, I'm not a full Witness yet, just a Regent. I'm still learning what I can and can't do."

"There are more people like you?"

"No, but there should have been," Shiloh explained, trying his best to dodge specific details. "I really can't go into that, sorry."

"What can you say?"

"There should have been more like me, but a long time ago a selfish man threw everything away, so I have a lot of making up to do. At first, I thought it would be easy, like in the movies, but when that guy tried to shoot your girls... well, that's why I got mad, I guess."

"So, is that it...why you're here? To justify your use of force?"

"I don't know. Maybe."

"The foundation of our civilization is based on the premise that vigilantism is the enemy of a judicial system. But..."

"Yes?"

"I've been trying to tell myself that you're just a vigilante who can fly, but I can't and it really bothers me. Witness, with the things you can do, you're going to have some hard decisions ahead of you. I probably won't like some of them, but you saved my reason for living, so if there is ever anything I can do for you, let me know."

Lisa leaned forward.

"And forgive me, I'm not trying to tell you how to do your job, but the real world isn't like comic books, if that's what you've been thinking. If you want people to take you serious, you're going to need to dress more seriously."

"Regent," Mattis interrupted.

"Just a moment," Shiloh said, holding up a hand.

"There is a situation in California; a hostage incident involving a member of Congress."

"I'm on it," Shiloh said to Mattis. "Mrs. Curtis, I've got to go, but I'd like to finish this conversation sometime. I have a few questions of my own."

"I'd like that."

"If you ever need me, just call."

"Call?"

"Pick up a phone and ask for me. Don't dial or anything, just ask for the Witness."

Shiloh hurled himself out her window. Lisa watched as he disappeared into the western sky and then sat down with her cooling cup of coffee to sort through everything.

All the cable news channels were carrying it: a hostage situation in California involving Congresswoman Minnie Rivers. On any given day, it would have been a national story, but it instantly became an international story when it was discovered that Congresswoman Rivers was the one holding the hostages.

Mattis kept Shiloh off the radar screens of a half dozen states as he passed through their air space. Shiloh reached San Francisco almost an hour after leaving Chicago. At the speed he was flying, the sun looked like it was slowly rising back into the sky, above the horizon, ready to set again. Twilight made it almost impossible for Shiloh to locate the scene. If Mattis hadn't projected directions to the site on his visor, he'd never have found it.

As he approached the scene, Shiloh could see the lights of dozens of police cars. It reminded him of his confrontation with Legion, except there were more media vans than police vehicles. During the time it took him to fly to California, members of the media had been alerted to the situation and had descended on the small clinic, readying for their appearances. Ignoring the life and death situation unfolding behind them, they practiced their plastic smiles and glued their hair pieces on.

A man in a thick blue bulletproof vest stood cautiously in front of his police car. Shiloh descended until he was a few hundred feet above the scene.

"Congresswoman!" the man yelled into his bullhorn. "No one needs to get hurt!"

"It's Congress*being*, you male chauvinist Nazi pig!" the obese gunman roared. "I'm Congressbeing Rivers the First and there is nothing for us to talk about! Either Congress unanimously passes my Global Earth Initiative or people start dying!"

"How did this start?" Shiloh asked.

Mattis instantly scoured every story on the situation and filtered out the fluff.

"The Congresswoman was visiting the clinic when, for no apparent reason, she grabbed a guard's gun and shot him. She took the others inside the clinic hostage and began issuing bizarre demands for their release."

"I've seen her on TV before," Shiloh said. She can't be any more incoherent than she usually is."

"She claims this clinic is her temple and she is cleansing it for her own second coming."

"Okay, so I was wrong. What are the police saying?"

"They are communicating on a private frequency, but are at a loss for a motive."

"How many hostages does she have?"

"Fourteen."

"Can you tell what's going on inside?"

Before Shiloh could finish asking the question, Mattis had scoured the internet, instantly locating thousands of photos of clinic employees, politicians who had visited the clinic; anything that had an image or description of the clinic's interior, including every database in California that dealt with it.

It assembled all of the blueprints, photographs and information into a three dimensional view. Shiloh saw the image of the clinic rotate until it matched his precise angle of vision.

Then the view changed.

Though fuzzy, the visual feed showed a grainy image of what was going on inside. Congresswoman Rivers was aiming her pistol at a woman sitting in front of her.

"How'd you do that? I can see through the walls!"

"It is one of the few tasks that actually require a considerable portion of my processing power. I am sampling the individual light photons that are escaping through the molecules of the wall and reassembling them into a coherent image."

However Mattis did it, Shiloh was amazed. Though blurry, he could clearly see the Congresswoman standing at the left side of the room. Except for the woman sitting in front of her, the rest of the hostages were back against the wall behind her.

"How fast am I?"

"Not fast enough to stop that woman from being killed."

"So I'm not faster than a speeding bullet?"

"Until you learn to harness the Witness power of Speed, your reflexes will simply not be up to the task."

"So people could die this time."

"People will die with or without your intervention, Regent. If it is truly your desire to stop that woman, you have been granted the power to do so."

Harley Song had been a San Francisco negotiator for twenty years, and was used to handling hostage situations. Berkeley had plenty of radical groups and over the past few years, hostage situations had become weekly infomercials for pet causes ranging on everything from the abuse of cockroaches in pesticide testing labs to groups protesting the human race and holding themselves hostage.

But in all his years, Harley had never seen anything like this.

What would make a senior citizen Congresswoman snap and take hostages? Harley was running out of time. He had to get the situation under control before the reporters turned on their cameras. He'd already filed enough protests to keep the Feds out of his hair for a few hours, but nothing was going to keep the media wolves at bay. He sent his best out to find anything in Rivers' background that would indicate mental instability, but her records had been recently classified; as recently as an hour ago.

Blasted Feds.

Harley almost choked on his bullhorn as a man silently lowered from the sky in front of him.

"What...?" he screamed, turning the bullhorn off. "Get down from there!" he shouted, but Shiloh ignored him.

"Stop that idiot!" Harley said and a dozen policemen tried to grab Shiloh's feet, but he was hovering just out of their reach.

"You're under arrest," one of the policemen said.

Shiloh looked down and almost laughed.

The policeman wore the traditional blue police uniform, but it was adorned with rows of flower shaped medals stretching across his chest.

All of the policemen were wearing them.

"The medals are rewarded for behavior ranging from 'Kindness in the Face of Bigotry' to 'Advanced Diversity Training'," Mattis explained.

The city had likewise taken their firearms away in exchange for community-friendly methods of discipline, leaving police with two weapons: plastic batons possessing the sturdiness of a cheap wiffle bat, and their ultimate weapon: a PETA-friendly taser. Designed not to discharge if accidentally placed against the fur of an animal, it was equally useless against hairy attackers.

Shiloh ignored the men and continued researching the inside of the clinic, so a couple of the policemen futilely threw their plastic batons at Shiloh. He didn't notice the batons, but he did notice that the Congresswoman had stopped screaming inside.

"What happened? She shut up," Shiloh said.

The Congresswoman was indeed quiet, drooling as she stared blankly ahead.

"She appears to be staring at you." Mattis said.

"Through a brick wall?"

"There is no other reason for her to be looking this high and in this direction."

Shiloh moved to the left and the Congresswoman's face turned to follow him. He moved to the right and she again followed his movements. When Shiloh moved closer to the building, she jerked back and shoved the woman she was holding toward the rest of the hostages. Then she raised her pistol and began wildly firing.

Ignoring the policemen below him, Shiloh crashed through the front plate glass window.

"Hey!" he yelled, moving between her and the hostages, waving his arms.

As Congresswoman Rivers turned to face him, her look of confusion momentarily turned to one of fear. Her lower jaw drooped open and a voice roared from her throat.

"*You don't belong here!*" she said, firing at him.

Shiloh instinctively raised his arms to cover his face. He still wasn't used to being shot at, but knew that he needed to provide as big a target as possible. Each bullet fell uselessly to the floor the instant they touched him. As Shiloh advanced, she turned her gun back to the hostages and Shiloh tensed and gasped.

Speed.

He needed to trigger the Witness power of Speed.

He knew it had something to do with holding his breath, so as he rushed toward the gun, Shiloh grabbed a breath, concentrating on moving fast.

It didn't work. The gun discharged and fire belched from the front of the barrel.

A thick woman in a purple robe fell backwards into a growing pool of her own blood.

Another bullet hit the wall behind the crowd, spewing dust.

Another bullet entered the leg of a pregnant girl in the back.

The last bullet struck Shiloh on the shoulder, splashing uselessly to the ground and Shiloh exhaled as he slapped the pistol from her hand. He heard a sharp cracking sound as the bones in her hand surrendered cohesion, but Congresswoman Rivers leapt forward, trying to choke him.

"This is not your world !" she bellowed.

Shiloh was confused. He tried to hold her arms to her side, but she was actually beginning to twist out of his grip. Shiloh tensed and slammed her against the wall and Rivers collapsed into the shattered brick. Though unconscious, her face continued to sneer and a low moan continued from her throat.

"There's no way she can be this strong," Shiloh said.

"She demonstrates the traits of a person possessed," Mattis explained.

Possessed? Shiloh tried to remember how he felt when he exorcised his friend Brad and touched the woman's face. He felt the heat as if it were a fever on her brow and concentrated. The heat raged for a moment and then the fire behind her eyes faded as a warm breeze blew past Shiloh's face.

The front door exploded open as the SWAT team burst through the door, passing the unconscious Congresswoman to surrounded Shiloh, aiming their rifles at his head.

"Are you kidding me? Help the wounded!" Shiloh said as he flew out the front window.

The men didn't know what to do, so they lowered their weapons and made room for the emergency medical technicians. One of the officers walked through the clinic's back door. After making sure no one had followed him, he lifted his head toward the sky and closed his eyes. A soft puff of smoke exited as he whispered.

"He is of the bloodline," the officer said and then disappeared.

Shiloh landed in an alley a few blocks away to calm down. He sat on the ground with his back to the wall. Although he planned to speak with the media after the hostage situation was over, he felt uneasy about facing them. He didn't expect Congresswoman Rivers to be possessed. And she spoke like she knew him.

What was happening?

"I can sense your anger and frustration, but you succeeded in stopping the assault."

"That's not the point, Mattis. I want to do it your way, but I'm so mad right now..."

"Are you any closer to mastering Speed?" Mattis interrupted.

"No, but I tried when I was in the clinic. I know it's somehow linked to me holding my breath, but it's not like flying. When I fly, it's like flexing a mental muscle. I can feel it surrounding me. This is... different. It's outside and I don't know how to trigger it."

"There is nothing in any of the histories concerning Speed other than the fact that it exists and that it manipulates the passing of time from the perspective of the Witness. But there is one thing you must always remember: if one Witness triggers Speed, all Witnesses enter Speed. If you do learn to master Speed, your brother Grayden will also enter Speed each time you do."

"I don't care. I need to learn how to trigger it."

"Speed is the rarest of all supernatural traits. Most Witnesses were never able to employ it at all. It is the sole ability that took your father years to master."

"I really didn't need to know that."

"Bit early for a Trek Wars convention, ain't it?" a voice interrupted. "Hand over the suit and all your money, space boy."

Shiloh turned to see four men, the first holding a large knife.

"Really?" Shiloh asked the sky. "Wrong night, guys."

"Hey Guido, he thinks we're his friends," one of the men said.

"Seriously, just go away," Shiloh said, irritated by the intrusion.

And then he remembered who he was.

"No, wait. You're the problem. You're why I'm here."

"This is the only problem you need to worry about right now, space boy," Guido said, waving his knife.

Shiloh stood.

The other men laughed and pulled knives. Guido, seeing the knives, put his away and pulled out a gun. Shiloh stepped forward and this time didn't flinch when the trigger was pulled.

The bullet splashed impotently to the ground, but in the dark alley, it was hard to see what happened, so they advanced. Their knives bent upon contact with Shiloh as the metal surrendered cohesion at the molecular level. The blades looked like they had been melted and then instantly refrozen in their warped state.

Panicking at the sight of their own weapons, the thugs dropped them and began fighting with their fists and legs. Though good fighters, their own bones took the brunt of the attack.

Shiloh grabbed one man by the leg in the middle of a kick, pulling him back fast enough to break the bone off inside his hip socket as he threw him at another of the men. They both collapsed into the wall behind them. He straight armed the largest of the men into the street.

All the while, Guido had been firing his pistol. After emptying his clip, he tried to beat Shiloh with it, but like his friends' knives, it melted around his hand and through his fingers as if the gun's molecules were retreating in fear of touching Shiloh. He pulled his hand back as if it had been stung, only to see it encased in a large glob of gun metal.

Guido screamed like a schoolgirl trying to shake the gun off his hand. Shiloh face palmed him and the bones in his face collapsed.

He wouldn't feel the pain until he awoke three days later. It would take a complex series of wires and putty to hold the basic shape of Guido's face together. The doctors would tell him he couldn't be fitted for dentures until surgery reconstructed his cheeks and jaw.

"Call an ambulance," Shiloh told Mattis and took to the skies, his anger still unsatiated. "This isn't going to be easy, is it?"

"The balance between power and rule never is," Mattis replied. "The frustration you feel will only grow stronger until you realize why you have been placed on this world."

"But this isn't Ehrets! Earth already has individual nations."

"Ehrets was a collection of nations before Arter united them."

"My Dad says that millions of people would have to die. Is that what happened on Ehrets?"

"No. At the time, the total population of our world was only two million people."

"If that's why I'm here, then how am I supposed to bring together billions of people?"

"There are thousands of possible scenarios, but that isn't what you're really asking, is it, Regent? You want to know if anyone would have to die for you to set up a world throne on Earth."

"And?"

"The answer is 'yes'."

Eating cereal fifteen minutes before midnight was not a typical way for Maria Phillips to spend an evening, but the past couple of weeks had been anything but typical. Her nightmares had become so severe that she feared going to sleep, so she had been staying awake until her body collapsed from exhaustion. But even then, sometimes the nightmares would come and she would awake, her heart racing and she would be crying so hard it hurt.

That's when she started taking her mother's sleeping pills. It was the only way she could fall asleep at a normal time. Maria grabbed three of the one-per-day pills and washed them down with raspberry flavored water. She reached for the remote. She needed the TV to occupy her mind until the pills did their work.

Maria had nightmares when she was younger, especially after her parent's divorce, but these were savage. They were the same every single night. The entire world was covered with a dark fog. She would be walking in crowded halls in school, but everything was in black and white like an old television show. And the others all had...things attached to them, smoky squid things with wispy faces and thin sooty limbs tearing at the kids' bodies, but no one seemed to notice.

Then she saw Shiloh.

The only person in her dreams that she ever saw in color, he walked by, ignoring her and everyone around her. After he walked out of the school, the smoky beings began killing everyone. Maria could never escape the building in her dreams. She had to force herself awake.

The first cloudy effects of the pills began taking effect when her television show was interrupted by a news bulletin. Couldn't they keep news isolated to the news channels? A reporter held his hand to his ear in the middle of a street somewhere in California. Maria laughed at the man.

He was wearing blue and brown together.

"Maybe I could get a job as a fashion designer for reporters," Maria dreamily thought.

"A hostage situation has just become something much more," the man said, in the bouncy tones of an excited child.

"Congresswoman Minnie Rivers had taken hostages at the offices of the Bright Future Abortion Clinic and negotiators were dealing with her when a man came out of the sky."

"Is this real?" Maria wondered. Had she accidentally switched to the sci-fi channel?

The video showed the front of the pink and yellow flowered abortion clinic. Maria took the last bite of cereal from her bowl when she about spit it out. The video showed a man hovering in front of the building. But it wasn't the fact that the man was flying that got her attention; it was the fact that Maria recognized the man's helmet.

It was the same helmet she had seen in Shiloh's room.

The cobwebs of sleeping medication were instantly burnt away. She set her bowl down and turned up the volume. Reporters with half applied makeup and wigs were scrambling to get their camera men to the front of the police line to get a clear shot. One of the older anchors, who hadn't yet put in his dentures, was screaming something unintelligible to his camera man who tried his best to decode the sound coming from the large flapping gums.

"Nina, the Windy City Angel isn't limited to Chicago. The new hero arrived late to one of the oddest hostage scenes this city has ever seen. A former hostage of the Congresswoman said that Rivers began firing on the hostages just before the caped man burst through the front window."

The scene changed to that of a middle aged man with a long graying beard, wearing a purple banyan. He had obviously been pharmaceutically thrilled prior to being on camera.

"Man, we're all huddled into a corner doing our tendai and she's screaming and then she starts shooting and this dude like crashes through the window, right? He has a cape and everything! Then Rivers starts belch talking some real weird stuff, man. 'This is not your world!' Everything happened like really fast. Pow! Pow! And she's firing real bullets! Heh, didn't even slow him down, man. He just walks up and one hands her through the wall... a friggin' brick wall!"

The man began giggling and the scene returned to the reporter, who was waving off the oddly dressed people gathered behind him. A shaggy girl remained standing defiantly behind, trying to hold up a peace sign with her fingers. It looked like she was giving the reporter bunny ears.

"Police say they don't know what motivated today's actions, but have arrested Congresswoman Rivers on one charge of reckless display of a firearm. Two of the hostages are in the hospital being treated for their gunshot wounds. Police have no comment on the actions of Chicago's protector. For WTN, I'm Rob James."

Maria's show came back on, but she turned the television off. It all made sense now. Shiloh recovering from the wreck so fast; his breaking Tony's wrist. She tried to concentrate more, but the rush of discovery had worn off and the sleeping pills kicked in. Maria collapsed onto her pillows, hoping that she wouldn't have any nightmares.

Her hope was in vain. Unlike her other dreams, when she opened her eyes, she was driving her car through a weird part of Champaign. She hadn't been there in a long time. She looked down and saw a caramel latte was in her right hand. It appeared to be a normal day.

Everything was even in color.

Then night came and her dream took her to a different city. She knew somehow knew she was in Joliet, though she had only passed through there once on the way to Chicago.

It was night and everything felt wrong.

She looked around for the smoky beings that occupied her every dream, but they were nowhere to be found. Maria parked her car and walked around, trying to find why everything felt so wrong.

It didn't take long.

The building she stood in front of exploded and collapsed to the ground in a cloud of dust and debris. Maria fell back to protect herself, but the debris passed through her. She walked back to better see what was happening when something erupted from the top of the rubble.

It was large and sharp and horrible; a dark creature covered with barbed joints. Its armor was a bulky slate gray metal that seemed to absorb light. Maria shrunk behind a piece of wall when the skull shaped faceplate turned to look in her direction.

She barely had time to digest the monster's appearance when something smashed it back down into the rubble.

Shiloh! It was Shiloh!

Maria watched with joy as Shiloh pulled the monster out of the wreckage only to pound it back into the ground. But as Shiloh turned the thing around, it sliced Shiloh with one of its barbs and blood spattered Maria's face. No matter what she did, she couldn't wipe it off. She looked up as the monster tore into Shiloh.

This was worse than any of her other nightmares.

Maria turned her face from the scene until the sound of a body slamming into the ground beside her forced her to look. It was Shiloh, bloodied and not breathing. The beast turned its attention toward Maria and this time, no matter what she did, Maria couldn't wake herself.

A bright light ignited a small patch of space just inside Jupiter's orbit, expelling a long plume of white matter followed quickly by a large gray cargo ship. It careened out of control, leaving a trail of ignited graviton particles in its wake. Though it was old enough to be nearly out of service, the vessel was hundreds of years more advanced than anything that could be found on Earth. But its sole occupant wasn't impressed with the technology.

In fact, he was cursing it.

Mosh clutched his harness as the ship's graviton field fluctuated, trying to recalibrate to the conditions of normal space. The cargo ship was bulky, designed for long hauls, not quick change, so Mosh braced himself as the center of gravity went from left to down to right to left and back. He passed dizzy and reached painful nausea in seconds. The G forces tore him from one side of his harness to the other until it became difficult to even breathe.

The ship thundered as it adjusted to normal space and the floor plates rattled in anger as they finally settled. Mosh cracked four ribs as he was thrown forward against the harness. He surrendered his last meal on Ehrets - the finest meal ever prepared for him in his rough life - slowly roasted verdure heart, covered in botanice peel and ancient herbal wine.

It came roaring up his throat, staining the floor in front of his comm panel. He continued shaking long after the ship steadied. It was nearly ten minutes before he had the strength to unclasp his harness.

But he had survived. He was alive!

A laugh came from somewhere deep within. Mosh had been a lowly mechanic on his home world of Ehrets, abandoned to the lower ranks by his twin brother Malthus, who occupied the office of High Priest. But even Malthus couldn't blatantly kill his brother, so he had sent Mosh off on a suicide mission: to penetrate a spacial anomaly.

Mosh laughed until one of the sensors began beeping. At first, he thought it was a malfunction. After he hobbled to the panel, he wished it was. Life support was being shut down to support a new command: Find and record everything on this side of the anomaly about the Regent Shiloh Mashal.

Mosh attempted to override the code, but he was a mechanic, not a programmer. There had to be a way to bypass the computer, but he had a more serious problem. He could already feel the cold touching the edges of his fingertips. There was enough breathable oxygen in the large ship to last months, but he would have to quickly find an environmental suit. The last fatality on one of his ships was a crew member who had frozen to death before he could reach his suit.

There were sixty lockers in the crew room, but only a dozen functional suits. Mosh slipped into the largest suit he could find, careful not to make any sudden moves. Though the material was a hybrid weave of nekosheth and mokbar, it was old and one small split would be enough to allow his body heat to escape. His suit instantly noted the decrease in environmental conditions and compensated.

Mosh disconnected the mainframe. The ship shuddered as main power shut down. The dull glow of ancient reserve lighting panels dimly lit the ship with their on again, off again blinking.

Mosh removed the mainframe panel and unplugged the largest of the biological matter packs controlling the unit.

It had obviously been used, but appeared to be functional. Behind it was storage space for two spares, but neither was loaded. Tossing the crusty bio pack on to a nearby shelf, he dug through shelves until he found a new one. It was out of place; still sealed and obviously never used in a ship where everything else was used and old.

Mosh plugged the new bio pack into the unit and connected it to power. The ship's lights instantly blazed to life and several systems began running routines. It was almost as if the pack had pre-programmed instructions. At that thought, Mosh cursed himself and raced to the bridge. The life support station was operational, but still shut down. Mosh manually overrode the switch and the panel itself powered down.

So, this was his brother's failsafe way to kill him. The other sensors were working, running various algorithmic programs searching for the Regent. The data was rattling off information filling every screen on the bridge.

The first thing it did was categorize the planet. Slightly smaller than Ehrets, the world had suffered a severe ecological disaster sometime in the past. Instead of Ehret's single continent, this world had seven shattered continents and no protective cloud cover. The radiation damage on the surface had to be tremendous.

Mosh returned to the mainframe. He left the new bio pack installed, but would have to find a way to bypass the lock on life support. The environmental suit would only last a few days.

Mosh grabbed the old bio pack he set aside and plugged it into the defensive grid. The shields immediately went down and the ship slowed to a safe speed to compensate. Before it could trigger the system incompatibility warning, Mosh disengaged the coupling and the panel powered down.

So far, so good.

He hadn't contaminated the old bio pack and the panel was still operational. Setting the defensive grid bio pack gently on a shelf, Mosh grabbed a portable generator and powered the panel to its base programming. The gray letters of the operational function screen appeared. Though defensive grids were primarily designed for shielding and internal gravimetric support, all major grids also carried backup programming for life support.

Mosh disabled primary functions and the screen went blank.

"Come on," he whispered, but the screen remained an empty black. Mosh slapped the panel in frustration, but nothing happened, so he turned the power up to operational levels.

The screen opened to a question:

ENABLE SECONDARY MODE?

"You better believe it!" Mosh yelled, punching in the code. The computer started new programs, routing primary life support to the defensive grid and Mosh sat back in his environmental suit and let out a sigh.

He had beaten his brother again.

After an hour, his suit display showed that temperatures were almost normal, so he removed the suit to recharge it. There was no telling when he would need it next and when he did, it would have to be fully charged.

It took several hours for Mosh to reroute the primary sensors' access to the power grid. He toggled a small switch below the primary control panel and it immediately began blaring a clarion warning. Thinking that it was malfunctioning, Mosh unplugged primary power to reset the panel, but when he plugged it in again, the sirens continued to wail.

Climbing out from beneath the panel, he checked the sensors. They were calibrated and functioning properly. Mosh had always prided himself in the quality of his work. His harsh life as a mechanic in the Toad Squad had saved his life. That placed him one rung above his fancy brother on the survival ladder. His ship needed a mechanic, not a priest, but the multiple system alarms worried even the mechanic in him.

The external sensors were detecting something bad. Alarms that loud were reserved for crashing into a planet or being pulled within a sun's gravity well, but navigational instruments showed that he was still on course.

Mosh switched to the external video display to find the problem. His mouth thinned in frustration. The screens at the stern of the ship were completely blank. Assuming that they were off-line or damaged, he called up diagnostic protocols.

All systems were operating normally.

Only when he looked at the stern sensors did the picture become clear; nothing could be seen behind his ship because something was blocking the sensors.

Something huge.

Switching all available sensors to monitor the rear of his ship, the mineral and magnetic sensors blazed to life. Numbers began chasing each other across the screen as if on some mad marathon and that's when the situation became clear.

Asteroids. He had materialized into an asteroid belt.

Worse, the gravimetric discharge upon exiting the anomaly had been large enough to break dozens of the asteroids' orbits and they had been following in his gravimetric wake.

Shields! He had taken down the defensive grid to jump start life support.

He was a sitting duck.

Mosh fired up the secondary fusion drive to escape, only to find out that the asteroids' path was so wide as to be impossible to avoid, so he bypassed safety protocols and set the fusion drive at one hundred and twenty percent, praying it would operate long enough to get the shields working.

He tore the panel off an auxiliary closet. At first he considered using the base panel, but rebooting from it would only reset the ship to space dock settings, and Mosh had already customized the vessel. As he had earlier prided himself on his ingenuity, Mosh now cursed himself for his pride.

He ripped out the primary panel controls and inserted the new controller. He had to turn off the fusion drive for a reboot and hoped the momentum he had gained would be enough to keep him ahead of the asteroids. The fusion drive and all primary power shut down as he rebooted the vessel's systems.

And the asteroids moved dangerously closer.

It had given up the ghost. That is, if there ever was any sign of life in Shiloh's old blue car, it was now gone. He had chosen the car over his dad's protests because it felt comfortable. Shiloh discovered that comfort doesn't matter when the engine is belching smoke.

Shiloh opened the hood, and a charred cloud flooded his face. Even though he could smell the smoke, he was somehow still breathing normal air. He coughed a few times for good measure in case anyone was watching. Shiloh waved the smoke away, futilely looking for the source of the mechanical trouble, but his knowledge of cars was limited to putting gas in the tank and handing his dad the oil filter every other month. Before his powers manifested, Shiloh had been too weak to do any sort of serious mechanical work, so he had ignored all the basic advice his dad had given him.

He heard a honk behind him. Shiloh pulled out from under the hood in time to see Maria's red sports car pull up behind him.

"Need a ride?" she asked.

"Yeah...to the junkyard."

"Hop in, I'll take you home."

Shiloh looked confused. Maria opened the passenger door for him, so he got in.

"That's a lot of smoke. Are you okay?"

Shiloh coughed a couple of times. It was weird having to fake a cough. He hoped it sounded authentic.

"I'll be alright."

"What happened?"

"It's dead. I spent two summers' worth of odd jobs for it and my allowance barely covers the gas these days."

"Sounds like you need a pick me up."

Shiloh didn't know what to say. Maria had made it clear about how she felt earlier, but she was literally in the driver's seat. They approached the coffee shop, but instead of pulling into the parking lot to go in, they pulled to the drive-thru.

"Chocolate delight?" Maria asked.

"Sure."

The drive thru box made human-sounding squawking noises.

"Two chocolate delights...venti," Maria said.

Shiloh stared silently ahead. He noticed the tension in the car as they pulled around to pick up the coffees.

"Is everything okay?" Shiloh asked.

"Fine," Maria said, handing him his coffee.

They drove toward Shiloh's house, but Shiloh noticed they were taking the long way home. Then Maria turned toward the park. Shiloh took a big sip of the too hot coffee, but it didn't burn. Maria removed the lid from her own coffee and blew on it.

"Is your coffee cold? We can go back."

"No, it's fine," Shiloh absently replied. He would have to be more careful about things like that.

"Good," Maria replied, hesitating about something. "Hey, did you see the news of that flying guy?" she blurted out.

"What?" Shiloh asked, caught off guard.

"The Windy City Angel, they have video of him in California! Did you see it?"

"No," Shiloh honestly replied. "Why?"

"I think he has a cool helmet. In fact, it looks exactly like the one you have in your bedroom."

Shiloh almost choked on his coffee.

"The last time I was over, Julie sent me to your room to look for your car keys and I saw the helmet and cape on your desk. I thought you were trying to get a Trek Wars costume for Halloween, but it's the same cape and helmet that he was wearing. That's pretty expensive stuff for a guy who can't afford to fix his car, don't you think?"

Shiloh wanted to run. His face flushed with the embarrassment of being trapped. Maria relaxed and continued.

"I wondered how you recovered so quickly from that wreck. I mean, Kristi's ribs are still healing and you're off your death bed like nothing ever happened. Breaking Tony's wrist totally freaked me out, but don't worry," Maria said. "Your secret's safe."

Shiloh took a long sip of his coffee. Maria smiled.

"So, tell me all about it."

Cornered, Shiloh didn't know what to do. So he told the truth.

"I'm a Witness," he said, hiding behind his large coffee. "Like Samson."

Maria's eyebrows raised in confusion.

"You know Samson, right? The guy who was super strong, but then they cut his hair and he lost his power?"

"What does that have to do with you?"

"Let's just say that I'm a descendant of Samson and I have his power and then some."

"So you're like Superman?"

"I wish."

"How did this happen?"

"I don't know how much I should tell you," Shiloh said.

"All of it," she whispered.

"I'll tell you a little and if you don't freak out, we'll go further. Stop at the park for a minute."

Maria pulled the car over at West Side Park. It was early enough after school that no one was on this side of the park yet.

"I'm serious," Shiloh said. "No one can ever know about this."

"I swear!"

Shiloh got out of the car and motioned for Maria to come out and sit on a bench. After she sat down, Shiloh casually leaned over to the front of her car, and not seeing anyone near, lifted it off the ground with one hand. Though Maria had expected something like this, actually seeing it took her breath away.

It was unreal!

And there wasn't even a hint of strain on Shiloh's face. He softly placed it back on the ground. Maria was giddy to the point that she almost clapped.

"Wow! Tony was lucky to end up with just a broken wrist!"

"I didn't mean to hurt him. I just wanted him to leave me alone."

"He deserved it!"

"Let me show you the most fun thing I can do."

"What?" Maria asked, waiting.

Shiloh stood there smiling, his arms stretched out at his sides. Maria was still waiting for him to do something.

"My feet," Shiloh whispered. "Look at my feet!"

He was hovering a couple of inches from the ground.

"Is that how you got to California so fast? What am I saying? Of course it is! Can you fly me around?"

"Well, I normally have to leave really fast so no one sees me. Maybe later."

Shiloh landed and sat next to Maria on the bench.

"So how did this happen?"

"Remember me telling you about Samson?"

"Yeah."

"The Samson of my world didn't fail his mission."

"Your...world?" she asked, stunned.

"Do you want to hear more?"

"You're asking a Trek Wars fan if she wants to know about life on another planet?"

"But this is real, though."

"So go on!"

"Our world is a lot like Earth. It's called Ehrets."

"Ay-ruts?"

"Uh, close enough. Anyway, a man on our world named Arter was given strength like Samson, but where Samson failed, Arter succeeded. His powers were handed down his family line. That's why I said I was a descendant of Samson."

"You're an alien," she whispered in her loudest whisper. "Do you normally look human?"

Shiloh's eyebrows wrinkled.

"I am human. This is me."

"So how did you get to Earth?"

"Long story, I'll tell you next time...if you want."

"We can guarantee that. Do your parents know?"

"Yeah, but no one else does, not even Julie or Tina, so you gotta keep this quiet."

"Cross my heart," Maria said. "Hop in, I'll take you home, but you owe me a ride now, you know."

Shiloh got in the passenger side, hoping he had done the right thing. All he knew is that Maria looked at him differently now and he liked it.

Shiloh strutted into his house. His mother, noticing the big grin on his face, closed her laptop. She was surprised to see Shiloh home; she hadn't heard his car pull into the drive.

"You're late," she pointed out.

"My car died at school."

"Your dad will be home in a few minutes. He can take a look at it. You look pretty happy for someone without transportation."

"Maria gave me a ride home."

"The same girl who just made you feel like dirt? Honey, you can't let girls play with your heart like that."

"She broke up with Tony."

"And why would she do that?"

"He was pushing her around. Besides, I told her...well, I guess she told me, really."

"Told her what?" Lillian asked, the glare on her face a sign that she suspected the truth. "Shiloh Wagner, what did you say?"

"Pretty much everything."

"Did she believe you?"

"Well, not at first, but I convinced her."

"Why, Shiloh?"

"She already figured it out. When she picked me up, I thought she was just being nice, but she cornered me about my helmet."

"How did she find out?"

"The last time she was here, she somehow saw it and after she saw the hostage situation on TV, she put two and two together."

The door opened, interrupting the conversation. George Wagner set his jacket down and sat down at the table.

"What's new? Learn to shoot marshmallows out your fingers?"

"Why don't you tell him what's new today," his mom taunted.

"Um, I talked with Maria Phillips."

"Is that good? Isn't that the girl you just broke up with?"

"Well, she broke up with me, but I, uh, I told her. Everything."

"You what?" George asked, eyes widening.

"Well, not everything."

"Shiloh, you can't tell every girl you like about your past."

"Why not? I'm a Witness, right? That's in my job description."

"I believe your job description is to witness about Someone Else. I don't believe you were given powers to impress girls."

"Can we trust her?" Lillian asked.

"We don't have a choice," George said.

"Sure we do! The only limitations I'm seeing are the ones that you're placing on me. You've never actually seen me do any of this stuff."

Shiloh stood from the kitchen chair and levitated off the floor.

Both of his parents jerked back a bit.

"Get down before someone sees you!" his mother whispered.

Shiloh landed in front of them.

"See? This isn't real to you yet! You know how big

our car is? I can throw it! I'm the strongest guy on Earth! According to Mattis, it's my destiny to rule this planet."

"Now wait a minute, Shiloh. We've been over this."

"My father ruled my home world as did his father."

"First off, I'm your father. Second, you once told me that your biological grandfather went crazy and it literally took an act of God to stop him."

"We don't have starving people or rampant sickness."

"Correct me if I'm wrong, but isn't Ehrets several hundred years more advanced than Earth?"

"Yeah."

"Then that has nothing to do with your ancestors; that's just a side effect of their advanced technology."

"But those advances were only possible because of the stable rule of one man. Look at how far behind Earth is compared to Ehrets! We started space travel centuries ago!"

"You're using 'we' a lot in referring to Ehrets."

"That's where I'm from!"

"But that's not where you are. Just remember that."

Shiloh glared and then ran to his room and slammed his door.

"I've never seen him like this," Lillian said. "What should we do?"

"Keep reminding him who he is, not who he was."

George Wagner solemnly entered his den. He wouldn't confide his fear to his wife, but Shiloh was changing and something needed to be done. But what?

And what could he really do about it?

As Andris Laima's nephew, Leif Laima had higher privileges than he deserved. Leif was a tag along relative who could never obtain his own living. He had managed to attach himself to his uncle Andris' religious empire at an early age right after his mother died. Starting as a second string bodyguard, he was replaced after diving for cover when some children set off firecrackers near him. He was a chauffeur until the third wreck. Leif finally found his true calling as a gofer. The one thing Leif discovered that he could do and do well was fetch, so Andris sent him around the world fetching.

Sometimes it was a person; sometimes it was just a piece of old paper. Leif traveled from Egypt to Brazil fetching whatever his uncle needed. That was when he received his first raise.

Some people whispered that Leif was mentally deficient, but he wasn't. Leif was just incredibly lazy. Besides, it didn't matter as long as he was successful in returning with the object in question, so Andris continued to send him out with first class tickets and a good paycheck, though Leif decided that he'd have to speak to his uncle about the food. He simply couldn't stomach airplane food, even as hungry as he was and the uptight pilots wouldn't allow him to bring his own food onboard.

This gofer mission had obviously been important to his uncle. So important that at first he'd hired a team of men to retrieve the object. But Leif caught wind of the mission. Andris grudgingly gave the job to Leif only after much begging. To show him just how important this mission was, he offered to pay Leif a hundred thousand euro bonus if he safely returned the object and told him that he would be fired "and worse" if he didn't.

It was an easy pickup, not like other times when he had to hire a personal bodyguard. He simply drove to an airport and switched satchels with a man and got on the next plane home.

Though he wasn't supposed to open the satchel, Leif had to see what was so important so he unlocked the case and looked inside. If someone discovered that he had opened the case, he would just tell his uncle that he was making sure the object was secure.

Inside the satchel was a piece of cobalt, the deepest blue crystal he had ever seen. It was shaped like a pyramid, about the size of a man's fist. A small eight pointed star was chiseled on each of the four faces and small, delicate characters were carved down each beveled edge. Leif wasn't supposed to play with it, but he liked the way the light spilled out in different directions as he held it to the plane window.

Turbulence knocked the crystal from his hands and it landed on the steel under structure of his seat and Leif cursed for the first time in his twenty-seven years of life.

Leif picked the crystal up and held it close to his chest like a baby, afraid to look at it. After a few agonizing moments, he pulled out his jeweler's glass and held the crystal carefully in front of him, inspecting every square millimeter.

Then he saw it...a crack!

It was tiny, not even half the size of a crumb. Even under the jeweler's eyepiece it was almost unnoticeable. Leif saw that it was under the corner, ending inside the etching of one of the bottom characters. Andris would never notice unless he was told about it, so Leif placed the crystal back in the satchel.

Before he landed, Leif received an urgent text message ordering him to hurry to his uncle's castle. Despite his hunger, he would put off lunch since his bonus depended on timely delivery.

When he entered the castle, he found his uncle standing in one of the garages near a suit of armor. Several men were prostrating themselves on the armor as if they were worshiping it. Their caresses were embarrassing, almost sexual in nature.

When Andris first began his new religion, Leif understood it was a front for something larger, but some of the people he had attracted were quite strange. Leif, as a dedicated lifelong Nothing-ist, wasn't going to waste any time wondering about the laws and rules of the new brotherhood.

But still, these guys were creepy.

His uncle had changed as well. When he was younger, Andris was best known as a gambling womanizer. But after his car wreck, he began attending séances and visiting mind readers. Leif's mother was Andris' older sister and she sadly whispered that Andris had gone mad; hexed by a gypsy. But Leif saw something in his uncle that he had never noticed before: a ruthless ambition that Andris turned into a full force religious movement. He had combined bits and pieces of major world religions into a mélange of theological thought. The broad appeal and rapid growth of The Church of Eternal Truths stunned the traditional churches in their native land of Latvia. It wasn't long before his new religion had a million followers.

Andris married one of his most wealthy followers and together they called themselves Brother and Sister Eternity. Their multi-million dollar wedding was broadcast live on most European television stations and that's when the donations came pouring in. Andris Laima was no more; to his millions of worldwide followers, he simply became known as Brother Eternity.

Andris took the satchel out of Leif's hands and carefully lifted the crystal from its case. Holding it to the light, the men instantly forgot the armor and walked to Andris, looking at the object as a child would his first Christmas tree. Each man's mouth was open in abject jealousy.

Leif tried to sneak out to grab something to eat when his uncle called.

"Leif, will you please disrobe?"

"Uncle?"

"We need someone to size the armor; it won't take a moment."

"Uncle, please. I haven't eaten a thing since before the flight," Leif explained and began to walk off.

"Leif!" Andris shouted.

Leif had only heard him shout once before and that memory was enough to convince him to humor his uncle and his odd friends, but this was the last straw. In the future, Leif would demand that his uncle provide better eating accommodations, or at least allow him the use of one of the private jets.

Leif removed his clothing and donned the odd looking wet suit. It was warm and stretchy and, Leif had to admit, quite comfortable. Andris motioned for him to enter the armor and as Leif settled in the chest cavity, the men began sealing the various compartments. A small wave of claustrophobia washed over him as the last plates locked in place. He tried to sit up, but the armor weighed so much, he couldn't move, so Leif inhaled deeply and closed his eyes.

"Leif, be still," Andris snapped, returning his attention to the men surrounding him. They brought the man who had stolen the armor. He had been beaten so badly he was too oblivious to protest their rough treatment of him. Leif only saw his shadow as it fell across his face plate. He didn't hear the man's gurgle as his throat was cut, only a faint thud as his body landed atop the armor.

One of the wizards, the only one to wear a traditional robe, poured the still-hot blood of the man over the joints of the armor. Leif recoiled as much as he could when the blood spattered over his face plate. The other wizards chanted at each joint and a small mist escaped as the life forces were drained from the blood, sealing the armor.

"Uncle! What are they doing?" Leif asked, raw panic crawling up his throat.

"Leif, be silent!" Andris commanded. "Is that the best you can do?" he asked the men surrounding him.

"No mortal could augment this metal any further," a tall man replied in a monotone voice that most Americans would recognize from his activities preaching about the dangers of global warming.

Andris checked the metal closely, looking for imperfections.

"This is the purest iron you could find?"

"The ore was imported from the finest Norse mines."

"Then everything is ready?" Andris asked.

An old man who tried to keep himself in the public eye long after his political career had died stood to his feet.

"All has been taken care of," he snapped in a thick southern drawl. "Magicks are like medicines; each has an effect and a side effect. A destruction spell augments the destructive capability of a weapon, but ruins a stealth spell. Detection enables you to see and hear further, but doesn't work with the mystical clatter of a destructive spell."

"I only asked for destructive and protective spells!"

The old man smiled his famous toothy grin, a smile that

at one time engendered trust. Andris recoiled.

"And that's exactly what you have received: the most powerful destruction and protection spells ever conjured."

"Did they interfere with the leash spell?"

"The leash is the prime spell, above and beyond all else. It will hold."

"What about the man inside? How will he live?"

"As long as he stays inside, he won't have to breathe or eat or drink or sleep, but the seals can never be broken. The man inside is forever lost."

A few of the wizards shook their heads at Andris' ignorance. Andris ignored them. Every society has its snobs. Ironically, in this setting, he was the hard working realist, surrounded by old blood magic and Andris didn't trust any of them. Whatever he needed to know, he had to find out now, but his questions were cut short as the last of his guests arrived.

Andris felt a tingle of excitement as the man entered the castle. He was only known as Meonemin and claimed to be three thousand years old. He was one of only two or three figures who were always mentioned with respect and fear in the supernatural world. Andris called in every favor he had just to contact the ancient mage.

It had taken Andris months before he found the small Bavarian village Meonemin called home. The guide who brought him ran back down the trail as Andris entered. Andris saw a frail looking man in an old wicker rocking chair. Still, Andris had learned not to accept what his eyes told him and prostrated himself before Meonemin, who appeared to be sleeping.

After Andris lit the candles on the floor before him, Meonemin stretched. The crack of a dozen bones echoed their dry snap in the small hut. Meonemin opened his eyes. His pupils were obscenely large and bright with the energy of youth. He looked at Andris as one would a stain.

Andris presented Meonemin with a dagger, an ancient artifact found at a burial site south of Mecca. Meonemin looked at it and tossed it behind him in disgust, grudgingly accepting the minor tribute. Only when Andris mentioned the USCHI project did Meonemin become interested. In fact, he had almost begged Andris to attend.

As Meonemin entered, the room of snobs instantly became subdued. The man certainly looked old, but no older than some of the others already in the room; certainly not three thousand years old. He was dressed more sensibly than most in the room. He wore no gaudy robes or large trinkets, simply a black suit, which starkly contrasted with his wrinkled, bleached skin and trimmed white beard.

He walked into their midst with the confidence of a drill sergeant, dismissing each of the men with his eyes. He smiled as Andris walked forward and they touched palms in greeting. Meonemin and Andris walked to the center of the chamber, directly behind the armor. Meonemin motioned for the others to stay behind.

"Knowledge is power," Meonemin spoke to Andris with a quiet rasp. "And I am a powerful man. I say to you, what occurs this day will change everything. This man shall become the herald for the gates of Hell, the eternal engine of destruction, the greatest weapon this world ever shall see. Should these men live long to see the USCHI triumphant, they shall prostrate themselves before you as ants."

Andris bowed before Meonemin.

"Stand," Meonemin whispered. "You are not the worm these others are. You are a man of greatness."

Meonemin waved his arms out.

"Come, Andris! Join me in the final incantations."

Andris allowed himself a smile of satisfaction as he

moved to the other side of the armor with Meonemin. The other wizards were motioned to come and they took subservient positions around the armor.

Leif couldn't hear what was being said, but it was obvious they were talking about him. And the way they looked when they glanced over to him wasn't good. Uncle or no, Leif had had enough.

"Uncle! I need to eat, let me come back later."

Embarrassed by his nephew, Andris nevertheless bent over and gave Leif his friendliest face.

"Leif, my friends are important people; the most important people I shall ever meet in this life and they can't stay long. Humor me and I'll tell Chef to make whatever you want."

The promise of food wasn't the same as food, but it was enough to take the edge off the gnawing pain that gripped the pit of his stomach. Leif tried to relax, thinking of roasted lamb and fine wine as the wizards began their final incantations. Over an hour later, Leif couldn't take any more. He rose from the slab. The movement was awkward, but he quickly adapted to moving in the armor.

"Leif!" Andris scolded.

"No, uncle! You can continue tomorrow!"

Leif walked away from the slab and pulled at the tabs sealing his helmet, but his fingers kept slipping off the latches, so he tried to pull off the right gauntlet. He pulled with all his strength, but the gauntlet wouldn't come off. Frustration quickly bled into panic as Leif realized that it wasn't just the gauntlets; he wasn't able to leave the suit.

"Uncle!"

Andris stared at his nephew.

"He won't need to eat?" Andris asked the other men.

"No, but you should have fed him before placing him in the suit. For as long as he lives, he will feel the hunger that now pains him."

"But he will live?"

"Of course."

Seeing Leif struggling to get out of his suit, Andris looked down in thought. After a moment, he nodded as an internal decision was made. Andris flipped a switch on the control panel and the armor locked in position as the power drained from it. Leif wasn't strong enough to move around in the suit when it wasn't powered and in his weakened and hungry state, was unable to do anything except fall with the suit. The armor landed on its face and Leif could see nothing but the stained stone floor.

"Uncle?" he whimpered, realizing for the first time what was actually happening.

"Uncle!" he screamed through the armor's speakers.

Andris turned out the lights and his party left for the mansion, leaving Leif alone in the garage. It was long past time for dinner.

The sounds coming through the speakers devolved from human screams to animal moans and finally sobs.

And then there was silence.

The scientists who created the Mattis series were only worried about one thing: that the units would get bored. So they dedicated almost a tenth of their programming to make sure that would never happen. No one had anything except theories on what would happen to a depressed artificial super-intelligence, but every scenario was bad.

Very bad.

Because of the potential threat of Mattis technology, the series was restricted to four units: Mattis, Healey, Gentry and Sumac, though the latter three were coded to be subservient to Mattis. One other difference existed between Mattis and the other units: Mattis' core directives had been rewritten before the Regent's launch that led him to Earth.

Programmers relegated the original list of directives to secondary status. Mattis was given three new sets of instructions, which took priority above all others:

1. *Protect the life and health of Shiloh Mashal at all costs.*

2. *Anticipate and prevent anything that might cause harm to the Regent, your programming or your functioning.*

3. *Investigate the disappearance of the Witness Imperium's brother Mossad Mataran until he is found.*

While Mattis' primary directive was to protect Shiloh,

actually obeying him was safely further down the list of directives. Prior to this, Mattis was a servant without a choice in its' own fate, but the new priorities truly opened the doors to Mattis' creativity.

Mattis had limited control over its own programming.

On a new world with a blank slate, there was plenty of raw information to sift through, from delegation of security checks on the Regent's identity to sifting through Earth history. Mattis had already set up an extensive library of databases comparing Earth and Ehrets.

Mattis was even allowed to make certain choices in its priorities. Small portions of unallocated time could be spent as it wished and when it first arrived to Earth, Mattis initiated a custom code which allowed 64-bit computing and anonymously distributed it to the programmers of industry leading software.

The new algorithms introduced shockingly powerful processing, providing personal computers access to things never before possible. No one asked where the code originated, certainly not the programmers who became filthy rich distributing it. But they noticed that the code only worked in one configuration, preventing them from altering it.

Only Mattis had the key to the core, which was layered programming of instructions on top of instructions on top of instructions. The mass of the algorithm caused another, invisible program to run and that program allowed Mattis to control any machine running it.

Nearly every computer built within the last six years now had the technology hidden inside. With the advent of 64-bit hardware, Mattis consolidated the algorithm, completing its control.

But despite the fact that Mattis had upgraded their technology, the total combined processing power of every computer on the planet was far less than a billion billionths of Mattis', which meant that the Regent's request for repair of their ship was futile.

The technology simply didn't yet exist.

The Regent had requested a new priority to conceal his identity and that required more than a passive program. To insure success, Mattis dedicated one thousandth of one percent of its processor time solely to the protection of the Regent's Earth identity.

One of the main subsets in Mattis' primary priorities was to protect the environment where the Regent lived; America specifically, and Earth in general. In the past seven years, Mattis had been able to route millions of dollars of various nations' budgets toward monitoring the skies for extraterrestrial life. That was just the ruse Mattis used to increase its awareness of anything out of the ordinary, whether an invasion from Ehrets or dangerous anomalies such as gamma bursts, asteroids and the like.

So far, Mattis had augmented the program to cover almost forty percent of the sky, though the rest of the world only had access to, and was aware of, six percent. Further synthesis of the program allowed a virtual coverage of sixty-four percent of the sky.

It was good, but not good enough. Mattis would continue until one hundred percent of the sky was covered, twenty four hours a day. It projected that true coverage wouldn't be possible for another eight years, but what Mattis saw in its hourly space checks made it seek avenues for accelerated development.

It detected a small group of meteors heading for a collision with Earth. Mattis piloted Shiloh's ship until it was close enough for short range scanners to study the situation. What Mattis first thought was a cluster of five or six meteors was in fact merely the first wave of dozens of meteors and asteroids. More importantly, Mattis detected something not seen on this side of the anomaly outside of their own ship; a gravimetric signature.

Mattis accessed its catalog of Arterran vessels and matched it to a series of cargo vessels used to transfer massive amounts of supplies to off world colonies. Had someone from Ehrets detected their signal and sent a supply ship? The timing seemed right. The signal sent nine years earlier would have reached the Ehrets system, but Mattis noted that the message would also have been received by Shiloh's insane brother Grayden and his army. As such, it constituted a threat to the safety of the Regent. Mattis partitioned its priorities, delegating a full percentage of its processes toward researching the cargo ship.

The vast majority of its processes were calculating the impact and solutions for the incoming asteroids, each reaching out into a billion different scenarios searching for a solution to stop such a large mass of asteroids.

Mattis piloted Shiloh's ship into a close intercept path of the front line of meteors and charged what was left of its weaponry. Sirens immediately began clanging, warning of the damage to the offensive arrays. Mattis ignored them and used the weapons until the system shut down and then bypassed safety protocols to force the weapons to continue firing. It was able to destroy over a dozen meteors before the offensive grid failed, but the last few meteors continued on their path and would hit the Earth within hours.

Mattis awoke Shiloh to give him the news about the meteors, but kept the information about the asteroids a secret until it could devise a plan to stop them.

The three lazy dogs that normally slept quietly in the shallow ditch in Niran Boonmi's back yard were no longer asleep. They were baying at the moon that shone brightly through the cloudy Thailand sky. Niran got out of bed and leaned out his window to clap his hands in anger. The dogs looked back and forth between him and the sky.

The sky won.

The dogs continued to bay even when Niran ran into the yard yelling at them. They only stopped baying when he tried to drag them to the back pen. Then they began growling. For a moment, he thought they were going to attack. He released their collars and they ran away.

Niran might have tried to chase them had it been daytime, but he was too tired from his sixteen hour workday. They would come back later, he reasoned as he returned to the small shack he had built.

He bought the land very cheaply from a widow three years earlier because an old shaman had told her the land was cursed. He didn't like taking advantage of an elderly widow, but he had to have a place to call his own before he could wed his bride.

Niran spent four months gathering scrap materials before he built the small two room shack. Only then did he bring his small dowry to ask for Chanakarn's hand in marriage. Her father looked at Niran's paltry sinsod and tried to barter for more, but Niran was adamant.

Seventy-two U.S. dollars or nothing.

After her father reluctantly agreed, Niran spirited her north to Chang-mai where he had arranged for three monks to perform their wedding with the extra eighteen dollars he had saved. His mother had told him that an odd number of monks ensured a good marriage.

They immediately moved into their new shack and Chanakarn became pregnant the first year with twins - a boy and girl - another sign of good fortune. And over the next two years, Niran's crops had been large. They forgot all about the old shaman's prophecy until he returned three years to the day that Niran purchased the property. As he had the woman before Niran, the shaman offered to dispel the evil spirits of his land for a fee, but Niran wouldn't listen. He had spent a few years in Bangkok as a teen and knew a con when he heard one. He spit on the shaman in disgust.

"Look around you, shaman; you stand on my land and breathe my air. Even the spittle that adorns your robes is mine. You can't scare us like you did the old widow woman. Now leave!"

"I raise a curse upon you," the shaman said, waving his ragged sleeves. "Three days and the heavens shall fall upon you and your family shall die on this land!"

Niran chased the shaman away and never saw him again. Chanakarn had heard what the old man had said and told Niran that he should have let the shaman bless the land, but Niran sent her back into the house.

That was two days ago.

On the third day, strange things started happening. Birds that had never been seen in Thailand came to settle on the roof of Niran's shack. Chanakarn claimed that she heard one of them tell her to leave with the children before sunset.

And now, the dogs began their loud baying.

Walking back to the shack, Niran heard other dogs baying in the woods and the forest came alive with animal sound in a way Niran had never heard before. Was it a coming typhoon or an earthquake?

It was said that animals could sense things, but he had never known an earthquake to hit the area and Chang Mai was too far inland to be flooded like Thailand's southern coasts. They would get occasional floods, but the sky, while cloudy, didn't show any of the anger that it typically displayed before a typhoon.

Then Niran heard a loud pop high above him in the western sky, instantly followed by a loud boom, and he felt a rumble as the shock waves reached the Earth. He looked up and saw clouds scatter in every direction. In the center was a star growing brighter and brighter.

Then he realized why the dogs were barking and the thought shook him fully awake. The star was headed right for them. Niran turned to race to his shack to awaken his family. His wife and two babies still slept inside. But the race to his house was over in an instant as the meteor obliterated his property, destroying everything and everyone inside. Niran managed to reach ground zero in time to be atomized by the explosion.

His dogs, which had fled in the opposite direction and escaped the blast zone, began the search for a new family as the land continued to shake beneath them.

Shiloh studied Mattis' projected path of the meteors as he crossed the Pacific Ocean and he knew he would be too late for the first two. Though it was night, Mattis was somehow manipulating the view in Shiloh's visor to make it look like day.

"Of the meteors that will survive entry into Earth's atmosphere, two will strike populated areas. The smallest will strike the Pacific Ocean. The first meteor has struck northern Thailand," Mattis explained.

"Why didn't we know about this sooner?"

"This world's stellar tracking systems are extremely limited and our ship's long term sensors are inoperable."

"But scientists are looking for stuff like this. How did it get through?"

"Even if your scientists had been viewing this area of the sky – which they weren't – they would never have seen these meteors. Using their naming conventions, they would be considered 'dark meteors'."

"What?"

"An astral body whose composition causes absorption or diffraction of light. I cataloged over eight thousand such objects upon entering this system."

"Have you told our scientists?"

"Indeed. I informed your government's top scientists, though until they see the phenomenon themselves, they will continue to say I should '*stop watching Trek Wars*'."

"This is taking too long."

"You can fly faster than this."

"I'm going as fast as I can."

"No, you are not. Look before you."

"There's nothing but the Pacific Ocean in every direction."

"Pick a spot on the horizon and will yourself to it."

Shiloh stared at a spot on the ocean at the very edge of the horizon and strained the mental muscle he used for flying to move to that spot. He felt a sudden, violent push, as if he were being shot out of a cannon.

Everything was moving too quickly for his eyes to adjust to, far too fast to control. Shiloh lost concentration at mach eight, tumbling out of the air, managing to catch himself before hitting the water.

"I can't go that fast."

"You have been averaging over three thousand, seven

hundred miles an hour. For the sake of the people of Thailand, you need to go faster."

Mattis plotted the incoming path of the second meteor in his visor and Shiloh pushed himself as fast as he dared, arriving in Thai airspace forty minutes later. He positioned himself below the path of the meteor while Mattis gauged the essentials.

"The meteor is seventeen meters in width, comprised primarily of nickel, iron and various silicates."

"Okay, what do I do, punch it or something?"

"It is traveling far too fast for you to attack. The only thing you can do is fly directly into its path and allow your Divine protection from kinetic damage to shield both you and the people below."

"That doesn't sound like a very good plan."

Shiloh held his position as the meteor approached. As it struck the atmosphere, it flared to life, scorching the air in its wake. And though he had tensed in preparation, Shiloh wasn't prepared for its raw speed. Before he could even instinctively place his arms in front of his face, the meteor hit.

But Shiloh didn't move.

The instant the meteor touched Shiloh, its momentum dissipated and it shattered. The shards that struck Shiloh lost their momentum, but immediately clashed with the few parts that had dislodged when it entered the atmosphere and were still following in the meteor's wake.

Large chunks of the meteor fell to the ground, devoid of their previous kinetic energy. The wall of heat washed around Shiloh, evaporating into the chill sky, leaving him dazed, but still hovering. Shiloh felt the damage being flushed out of his body, but he could still feel pain in the deep areas of his bones.

"Regent, are you alright?"

Shiloh was stunned by how fast it had all happened.

"Did I stop it?"

"You dissipated its momentum enough so that the remnants are only causing minor damage. Local officials have been notified."

Shiloh looked down. The meteor's debris had started several fires in the Thai jungle. He considered stopping the fires for a moment before the pain washed over him again. Shiloh could tell that each time he was feeling better, but all he wanted to do now was get to bed and it was a long trip home.

"How many more are there?"

"When our ship detected these meteors, it was able to destroy several before they reached the atmosphere. Due to our lack of long range sensors, I sent it out further. It has detected a swarm of asteroids headed our way."

"Can the ship stop them?

"The ship was able to stop over a dozen meteors before the offensive grid went off line. It was severely damaged during the passage through the anomaly."

"But our technology is so far advanced. Is there anything we can combine with what we have here on Earth? Can't we just amplify some nukes or something?"

"Earth science is still centuries behind Arterran science. Their scientists are just discovering what you call 'dark matter'. Once they come to understand the nature of energy and matter in the coming centuries, they will discover the negative forces: anti-gravity, nuclear, magnetic as well as the parallel forces. But until that point, there is nothing of technological value on this world."

"There's got to be something we can do."

"It would be like trying to repair your personal computer in the year 1200 A.D.."

"We're that far behind?"

"At the very least. Now, return home and get some rest."

The majority of the asteroids were safely enough behind him that Mosh could spend time sequencing the shields. He was a mechanic, not a technician, familiar enough with the principles of shield technology that he could set them up, but he was running out of time.

Mosh took a seat at the main console. The computers continued to run their programs searching for the Regent, but he managed to route one of the minor units to work on the shields. Mosh looked at the screen while waiting for the shields to resequence. Images of the Regent's world showed that it was raw and bare. The planet's cloud cover was all but gone and the mother continent had been shattered into smaller landmasses, scattered across the face of the planet, but Mosh looked longingly at the images.

This was going to be his new home.

Mosh sat back. He couldn't stop the computers from their gathering duties, but he didn't care. They could record until the End of Days. His brother Malthus hadn't given him death; he had given him a new life and freedom... freedom from the Ehrettan caste system, far away from every chain that had ever been placed on his life.

Odd.

Mosh could access the search program, though he couldn't halt or change its operations. There was no indication that a Witness ever existed on this world. Hundreds of nations separately ruled their own small parcels of land. But even if this world had no Witness (*a concept Mosh secretly wished for while growing up, but still found hard to grasp*), the Regent's powers should have manifested by now.

Yet there was no indication that he was ruling or attempting to do so.

In fact, as Mosh looked through the logs, he found so many fictional accounts of Witness-like scenarios that the programs hadn't yet found any real information about the Regent. In every media format available on this world, there were thousands of super-human events.

But none of them were real.

What kind of world was this? It was a planet without a Witness, but crying out in every way it could for one. Even with a cursory glance of the database, he saw that many people on this world were dying of starvation and disease. The richer nations had dedicated the majority of their money and effort into methods of entertainment. They were so hungry for a Witness that they had to make up fictional stories to assuage their subconscious desire.

The ship's emergency beacon activated.

"Lotta good that does here," Mosh mumbled.

He must have accidentally reconnected one of the console ports that controlled communications. The beacon transmitted its signal in all directions. It took several minutes to reach Earth, where only one computer was advanced enough to decode its signal.

A light began blinking on Mosh's communications console.

"*Odd*," he thought. Since he believed that there was no one to communicate with on this side of the anomaly, he ignored it. He couldn't ignore the main screen turning on, however. The royal emblem of the House of Arter was displayed in the center of the screen. Mosh thought it was a malfunction until he heard a clipped baritone voice.

"Identify yourself," the voice said.

"I'm through taking orders," Mosh said, not turning his attention away from his work. "But I'm curious as to who you are, though. Nothing on that little planet I saw has the marzelvanes to override my protocols. Is this the Regent?"

"I am Mattis Prime, a synthetic personality designed by the Witness Imperium, Eythan Mashal."

"*The* Mattis unit?" Mosh asked, setting down his tools and looking at the screen. He was told the original Mattis unit had been destroyed, another of his brother's lies. "What do you want?"

"As you are aware, there is a cluster of asteroids heading toward this planet. If it is your intention to live on this world, we share a problem."

"Where's the Regent?"

"This particular problem is beyond his capacity to solve."

"So he *is* alive."

"Yes. Have you detected the nuclear warheads that are heading your way?"

"I thought this might be a civilized world until I saw those things."

"They are the most powerful weapons available to this culture."

"Those old atomics won't do anything against these asteroids. And if the Regent can't stop them, I don't know what you think I can do."

"In a show of good faith, I have disabled a number of sequences that were hidden in your consoles' programming. Left unchecked, they would have detonated the power supplies stored in your cargo bay, killing you after finishing its fact gathering mission."

Mosh muttered a curse and set down his tools.

"Okay, you have my attention."

"I propose that we take the power cores on your ship

and connect them to the retroincabulator on the Regent's ship. The ships would have to be stationed past the first two asteroids, closer to the larger mass, where the cores would be synced to overload, triggering a massive gravimetric well."

"Wait, aren't you forgetting something? If those first two hit, it won't matter that the rest miss."

"The Regent is taking responsibility for the first two."

"Really? According to all of the programs this ship is running, he hasn't taken responsibility for anything yet. You really think that kid can handle a couple of mountains like that?"

"Of course. The waves generated from the gravimetric detonation of our vessels should not only destroy several of the other asteroids, but also create a gravity well strong enough to change the paths of the remainder."

"Sounds like a plan, but why do you think I would commit suicide to help you?"

"Your safety would not be in question. You would merely be responsible for physically connecting the power cores and linking the ships. I will take control of both ships, depositing you safely on Earth before sending your ship back out to rendezvous with the Regent's ship to detonate the gravity well."

"I still haven't heard a reason to help you."

"Survival on the planet Earth."

"Errf?"

"Earth. My offer stands; what is your response?"

Mosh would need help getting acclimated on the planet. If their technology was as far behind as his sensors had indicated, it would be rough living there and he'd had enough of that.

"Deal, but only on one condition. Since you were made by the Witness' hot shot scientists, I'm sure they put enough marzelvanes in you to override anything that exists on Uth."

"Earth."

"Whatever. Can you override their technology?"

"Of course, but why do you ask?"

"I want you to set up an identity for me. I'm helping to save it, that's not too much to ask."

"That is an acceptable condition. We can negotiate the specific terms later. Now, we must..."

"No, we negotiate now. Living hundreds of years in the past isn't going to be easy. I want to be rich, but not too rich. I mean, I don't want to attract any attention. And I want you to program their language and customs in me. You can do that, right?"

"Yes. I will just need to input the coding into your medi-bay."

"Then start programming. I'll send the security protocols so you can access..."

"That isn't necessary; I bypassed your security before contacting you."

"Whatever. Don't forget, I need your ship's schematics."

The screen went blank. Mosh didn't know if this would even work. He would be sacrificing his ship and be stuck on...what was it called?

Errf?

If the plan didn't work, he would be just as helpless and die along with the other people there. But what other choice did he have? The cargo ship he was given was stocked mostly with machinery, not food. Besides, he would die in a couple of weeks anyway, either by asteroid or sabotage.

The main console lit up again.

"The sequences have been entered into your medi-lab. Just run the cultivation program. Your navigational panels have been reprogrammed to allow maximum speed. You will accelerate to Earth past the first wave of asteroids. We are running out of time."

"You just be sure that when I get there I'm set up."

Mosh activated the thrusters and the cargo ship roared to life. The superstructure shuddered for just a moment as it reached maximum velocity. Mosh glanced again at the read out of this new world. It held the promise of a new future away from his murderous brother and the insane Grayden, away from the Toads.

Maybe even a happy life.

It was worth saving, Regent or not, but he wasn't going to let Mattis know. Mosh brought up the schematics to both ships. Obviously Mattis had been able to access his onboard sensors to detect his cargo. That's the only way he could have known about the extra power cores.

Looking over the specs of the Regent's royal cruiser, Mosh whistled. Even after a decade, it was the nicest ship he had ever seen. Checking the logs, he noted the ship's extensive damage. It had taken quite a beating, but was still functional for transport and that was all he needed. The central power core was missing, but the reserves were fully functioning.

This could work.

If he rigged enough of the power cores to detonate in the path of the asteroids and both ships overloaded their gravimetric drives, it would generate an independent gravimetric field, hopefully strong enough to change the asteroids' paths. The tricky part was aiming the field where it wouldn't warp any of the other local planets' orbits.

Mosh calculated that the field would last a bit more than three weeks and then slowly dissipate. But if it was placed in front of the most damaging of the asteroids, it wouldn't have power to move the others. There was no way around it; the machine was right. The ships would have to detonate behind the first couple of asteroids.

The first two would be up to the Regent. Mosh walked to the ship's small medi-bay and placed the scanner on his head. An hour later, the program powered down and Mosh staggered to his feet, sorting through the new information that had been added.

"It's called 'Earth'," he said, in proper English.

The steam from the pot of boiling flesh clung to the walls of Andris' prayer chamber like a sticky fog. The human stew sickened his stomach and he had to fight the urge to gag with each salty, stringy spoonful, but he was somehow able to finish the warm bowl and set it on the red chalk outline at the top of the eight pointed star before him.

It was another vital step toward power. Humor the gods to gain power; suffer physically to be rewarded spiritually. Andris placed a candle inside the empty bowl and lit it. The Oracle appeared inside the shadows cast from the flickering candle.

The empty maw of the eye sockets silently locked onto Andris with its enigmatic stare.

Normally, Andris' sacrifices gave the large face a glow of glee, but today, the face looked down in stern condemnation. Andris felt awkward before the stare, but continued the ceremony.

"I have prepared as you have asked: *'a meal from the dead only a son may eat'*," Andris said with a formal bow.

Silence.

The Oracle didn't even bother to look at the exhumed body of Andris' mother still bubbling in the large pot at the back of the room. It merely continued to glare.

Andris ignored the stare and sat patiently. Their time was limited, but the Oracle had never failed before.

"What has my sacrifice purchased?"

The silent stare continued for several seconds.

Andris' stomach began clenching and churning as acid rolled its way up his throat. The sickly sweet smell of formaldehyde that clung to his robes didn't help.

"This is the sacrifice you called for. I ask again, my Oracle, what has that sacrifice purchased?"

The face continued to glare at Andris for another minute before his patience began wearing thin.

"Is it the USCHI project? You never answer questions when they pertain to USCHI."

"That which is known to you as USCHI is not known to you."

Andris could feel the air start to shimmer and knew that their session would soon end. He was running out of time for politeness. One of the first things he had learned in the supernatural world was the same lesson he learned in the business world: services paid were services to be rendered and even beings as powerful as the Oracle were bound by supernatural agreements.

Besides, the Oracle's demands had gotten more sadistic with each session. He couldn't imagine what would be demanded if they were to have another. He didn't even want to think about it.

"Our time is nearly over and you still have not given a prophecy!"

"Then listen carefully, mortal. From the book of the N'biy: In those days, the sons of Arter shall come to make war with the son of Samson. And their war shall cover the Earth and fill it with earthquakes and plagues and diverse disasters. The moon shall grow red and the stars shall fall from the skies. The nations of man shall rise to battle and fall in death."

Andris absorbed the words, but then his anger flashed.

"That's not a personal prophecy!"

"It is from a book you are not worthy to read."

"I paid for a personal prophecy! I demand the words that my sacrifice has purchased!"

The face bristled, contorting its bony jaws. Andris thought he saw something wriggling beneath the ivory surface of the Oracle's bony face.

"Demand? From a mortal who calls himself Brother Eternity yet does not know his own time or place...you cannot demand."

The Oracle moved directly before Andris' face and the room began to slowly shake. Andris was intimidated, but didn't back down. He held the cards in this situation and he knew it and he wasn't going to let the Oracle distract him until their time ran out.

"You have been paid and now you must give me a prophecy!"

The Oracle's face contorted in anger.

"You wish for a prophecy?"

"I paid for a prophecy and you will provide me with one! I am your overseer! In this room..."

"Nawbaw..."

In the roar that filled the room, Andris didn't catch the last word, but even if he had, he would have never understood the Arterran command to prophesy.

"...I am your master!" Andris taunted.

The face cracked a cold-blooded smile as the words almost tangibly reverberated around them. They filled the chamber, as much a part of the room as the air that Andris suddenly found hard to come by. He fell to the floor as his words surrounded him.

The Oracle's dark eyes stretched wide open as it spoke and for just a moment, Andris saw small pinpricks of crimson light dancing at their center.

"Your final prophecy is paid with the fruit of your own tongue. The last words you shall utter before your death will be 'I am your master'."

The Oracle disappeared, leaving Andris alone with his words.

It didn't take much convincing from her mother to have Julie take Tina shopping. A "sister-to-sister moment," she said, handing Julie two months' allowance. Had Julie understood why her parents really wanted them out of the house, she never would have left.

Shiloh and his parents were sitting in his father's locked den and Mattis had forwarded his signal to the ever present laptop on George Wagner's desk.

"You sure that no one else can get this?" George asked.

"No one on this planet possesses the technology to decode my signal," Mattis explained.

"So why are we here?" his mother asked Shiloh.

"You know how Mattis is always telling me that I'm not supposed to be stopping small things? I got my first official 'Witness job' from him today. A bunch of asteroids are headed toward us, so I'm going to stop them."

"Honey, asteroids are almost small planets."

"Yeah, a few of these are kinda large."

"How large?" his father asked.

"The largest is six miles wide," Mattis replied.

"Wait, a few?" George Wagner asked as his mind attempted to process the information. "How many are you talking about?"

"Don't look at me," Shiloh said, holding up his hands. "Mattis?"

"There are three waves of projectiles headed toward the Earth. The first wave consists mostly smaller meteors and debris. The second wave contains two large asteroids. The final wave is a massive field of asteroids and meteors that measures six thousand miles wide."

Shiloh leaned forward to reassure his parents, whose faces were turning white.

"Don't worry. Mattis said that if everything works out right, I'll just have to handle the first two asteroids."

His mother glared at him.

"Shiloh, asteroids that large killed the dinosaurs!"

"Actually," Mattis interjected, "Your dinosaurs and most of the larger species were destroyed by a world-wide flood. Dinosaurs still exist on Ehrets."

His mom covered her mouth. "Does the government know?"

"I immediately informed your government about the threat as soon as it was discovered. I am also assisting them in covering up the existence of the asteroids to prevent panic. No nation can see that part of the sky. Those countries that have telescopes that can monitor the situation are now experiencing technical difficulties until the problem is addressed. Your government has already launched multiple nuclear warheads toward the first two asteroids, but it won't be enough."

"How many asteroids are we talking about?"

"One hundred and twelve."

"My God..." George whispered.

"That would destroy...everything," Lillian said.

"Hello, resident superhero here," Shiloh interjected.

George looked at Shiloh in disbelief.

"Remember when you told me how much it scared you when that man shot you? That bullet maybe weighed a few ounces and traveled about nine hundred miles an hour. Asteroids are the size of a mountain traveling a hundred thousand miles an hour."

"I stopped the meteor just fine."

"I seem to recall you being in quite a bit of pain."

"My dad said that he could move a mountain if he needed."

"But he was the senior Witness or whatever. You don't have his level of power."

"He was Witness Imperium and I'm all we have."

"You know what I'm saying. You don't have all of his power."

"Ever since I got these powers I've wanted to make a difference; to do something big. This is why I was sent here, to stop stuff like this."

"Shiloh, I don't think you have any idea how dangerous this is."

"We have help," Mattis added. "I recently detected an Arterran ship en route to Earth and have convinced the pilot to assist us in diverting the last wave of asteroids."

George sat up straight.

"Is he trouble?"

"His name is Mosh. He was sent here on a suicide mission by the High Priest. It is highly likely that he was also sent here as a form of punishment. His logs show that no thought was given toward his care. In fact, multiple devices were installed to kill him after the mission was completed."

"What was he sent here to do?" Shiloh asked.

"To gather and then send information concerning you back to the High Priest."

"You said they thought I was dead!"

"The emergency signal that was sent after our passage through the anomaly must have just reached them."

"Are they coming for me?"

"I do not know."

"Can we trust Mosh?"

"Of course not. But his ship is a vital part of this plan."

"How?" Shiloh's father asked.

"We are currently joining technology from both ships to create a gravimetric field just inside Mars' orbit. It will route the majority of the asteroids out of Earth's orbit and into the sun."

"Can I talk to him?" Shiloh asked.

"It is not advisable. The less he knows about you, the better."

"C'mon, Mattis; I'm not going to invite him to dinner."

"I strongly caution against it. You don't have much time before you have to leave."

"Exactly why I need to talk to him. Look, if it gets out of line, tell him the reception is bad and we can talk later."

"Only on the condition that the Wagners refrain from speaking. He does not need to know anything about your home life. Are we agreed?"

George looked at his wife. She nodded.

"Agreed."

It only took a moment for a slight gravelly voice to come over the speakers.

"Now what?" the voice, obviously aggravated, asked. Even though the words were spoken with a British accent, it gave Shiloh a chill to hear someone from his home world.

He smiled.

"The Regent wishes for a moment of your time."

"I'm kind of busy," Mosh replied. Then Shiloh heard a sigh as something metallic was set down. "Okay, hurry."

"Hello. This is Shiloh Mashal."

"I kinda guessed that. What do you want?"

"I just wanted to talk to someone from home. How are things there?"

"How do you think? When Grayden took over, he wanted things to go back like they were, but everyone knew he'd killed your father. There were mass riots until Malthus turned the Enforcers loose."

"Enforcers are Arterra's mechanical army," Mattis explained. "Malthus is Mosh's twin brother."

"My non-identical twin and he's scum," Mosh added. "After a few thousand people were killed, the rest of us got the idea that this was how life was going to be, so we just keep our heads down and fit in."

"No one's fighting him?"

"Kid, no one *can* fight him. You know how strong you are? Well add a few thousand armored androids as your personal security force and the most powerful supernatural weapon in existence and see how long the people on this world would fight."

"What about General Maugaine?"

There was a cold pause followed by the sound of Mosh spitting.

"That coward ran when everything went bad."

Mattis remained quiet. Though it knew the true story, Mosh was still not to be trusted and would be kept in the dark as to any information concerning General Maugaine.

"He was my father's strongest supporter!" Shiloh said.

"Don't let that machine fool you, kid. There are lots of stories I bet it hasn't told you. Maugaine doesn't support anyone but himself. He came with all kinds of promises, but when something bigger came along, he ran. No one believed in him more than me. Other people turned their eyes so he wouldn't judge them, but I thought they were just being superstitious. Then I started to hear about him executing people on his own authority. If he thought you crossed the line, he'd kill you, he'd kill me, and he'd kill everyone in your entire family."

"I don't believe you."

"Believe it...he executed a dozen people with his bare hands, including your grandfather."

"What?" Shiloh asked.

"No one told you? Your grandfather Rawshah was the Witness Imperium before your father Eythan. Maugaine killed him like a dog in the same Temple where he spent half his time praying. Blood is always going to be on that man's hands and where ever he is, I'm glad he's not here. As far as I'm concerned, he's no better than Grayden!"

Shiloh's mind raced. Mattis had told him that it took an act of divine intervention to stop Rawshah, but he didn't know that Gerah Maugaine killed him... and with his bare hands? What kind of a man could do that?

Images from his childhood flooded to the surface and Shiloh shivered as he remembered Gerah's unyielding eyes.

"We will let you return to your work with the thanks of the Regent," Mattis interjected, sensing Shiloh's confusion.

"I've still got a lot to do. You just make sure you hold up your end," Mosh said and ended transmission.

"Mosh doesn't know the whole story..." Mattis began.

"What did he mean when he said 'hold up your end'?" Shiloh interrupted.

"We forged a deal. He gives up his ship to help save the Earth and I will establish an identity for him. It is how he is able to speak English."

"So you just give him a bunch of money and stuff?"

"Along with a number of properties and frills, yes."

"So he's not doing this out of the kindness of his heart?"

"Hardly. Mosh belonged to the lowest tier of Arterra's caste system. The Toad Squad, as they are called, performs the work that machines can't or aren't allowed to do. Living a rich lifestyle is the ultimate dream for such a person and while Earth's technology is several hundred years behind Arterra's, his life here will be far more comfortable than what he left."

"Why didn't you tell me about General Maugaine?"

"I have summarized much of the history of our world."

"So what specifically happened?"

"Records are scarce concerning the first appearance of General Maugaine, but it was recorded that your grandfather Rawshah had gone insane and banished his first son Mossad, from the throne, which is how your father as second born, inherited the Regency. When he could no longer ignore his father's insanity, Eythan formed an army to fight him, but no army is a match for a Witness Imperium and Rawshah had been very well trained in the use of his powers.

He ignored the army and attacked your father. Somehow, your father survived the attack and fled to the Temple to pray for deliverance. Rawshah was attacking your father when General Maugaine arrived. He killed Rawshah with the Sword of the Death Angel - not his bare hands - and helped your father restore trust in the Throne of Arter. Without General Maugaine's direct intervention, your father would have been killed and you would never have been born."

"So is he a good guy or a bad guy?"

"There are arguments for both sides. By his own admission, General Maugaine exists outside the laws and morality of men, including the rule of your father. Mosh was correct about one thing; General Maugaine was known to pronounce judgment on people, executing them on his own authority, sometimes directly counter to your father's wishes. But those cases were rare and involved dangerous people."

"Then why did my father let him hang around?"

"Your father counted Gerah Maugaine as his most trusted ally, above any man on the planet. Yet he also knew that if he were to violate Divine Law that General Maugaine would punish him."

"That makes no sense," George interrupted. "To keep

someone who believes he has the authority to be judge, jury and executioner is insane."

"George Wagner, Ehrets is an alien world to you in more ways than you can imagine. But realize this; the men of our world are similar in nature to the men of this world and if Samson had not thrown away his mission, your world would be more like ours than you care to admit."

"Look, I may not be a super-smart computer, but I know people and allowing someone to have that much power is simply insane."

"Is it 'insane' just because you don't understand the reasoning behind it? Mr. Wagner, the Creator Himself gave Gerah Maugaine his power. My reasoning algorithm is based on the premise that any decision by the Creator is by definition sanity. Reasoning counter to that would fit the definition of insanity."

George sat back, clearly unhappy, but he thought about Mattis' words.

"This discussion can continue later. Regent, you need to prepare to leave."

Mattis signed out with its signature blip and Shiloh turned to give his parents a hug.

It was time to go to work.

Julie hated her parent's car, but it was the only working vehicle in the house. Besides, Shiloh's car was worse, even when it was working. The only reason she ever took it was to show her parents that she didn't have to rely on them for everything.

And she didn't. Her part time job at McBurger Queen paid for some of her clothes and she got to work with a lot of her friends, so it wasn't that bad. But one of the prices Julie had to pay to have driving privileges in the Wagner house was as occasional gofer in case of small emergencies and her Mom pulled rank at least twice a month. And this time, her Mom insisted that she have a "sister night" with her nine-year-old sister Tina.

She used the excuse of having to go to the store to take her little sister on a big night out. Her mom gave her some extra money to spend time with Tina, so Julie agreed to take her to a movie. Besides, they never really hung out because of their age difference.

Julie wished she had an older sister when she was young. She had been an only child - about Tina's age - when Shiloh came along. He seemed so weak and fragile that Julie was afraid to play with him. So when her mother approached Julie about sneaking Tina out for a sister outing, she gladly accepted.

Julie took the long way around, outside the city limits to an old county road that ran parallel with the loop. For sure, the route was much slower, but it gave her time to talk with Tina 'girl to girl'.

"Why are we going this way?" Tina asked. She had been to the All-Mart a hundred times, but had never gone this way.

Julie had.

When she first learned to drive, she purposely took the long way around so she could have more driving time. The corn fields stretched north as far as she could see. If conditions were right, she could even see the faint tip of the Fisher grainery from the top of the hill, but today wasn't such a day. An earlier rain had begun to evaporate and heat waves danced on the small county road, making everything wave in the distance.

Then she saw something blocking the road ahead.

Visibility wasn't poor, but it was bad enough that she couldn't make the object out clearly. It was tall and white and it reflected what little sun appeared through the clouds. Whatever it was, it wasn't moving out of the middle of the road at the approach of her car so she slowed down.

"Sit back," she told her sister. There's something up ahead."

Tina leaned forward to see what her sister saw.

"I said sit back!" Julie barked.

When she got closer, she saw that the object appeared to be floating above the road. The wavy heat must have been playing tricks with her eyes. But she soon saw that they weren't. The object was clearly hovering above the road.

That's when it turned around and Julie saw that the shiny thing she had noticed was a helmet. It was the man the news had talked about.

The Windy City Angel.

Julie stomped on the brakes and the car swerved to a complete stop. The move didn't startle the floating man, but it did get his attention and he floated toward their car.

Just before he reached her, he smiled and waved at them and tore into the sky.

"Julie! It's the angel, Julie! See him? He can fly!"

He was gone in an instant, leaving Julie wondering what she had really seen.

Shiloh smiled. Even though it took a few extra seconds out of his appointment with the meteor, it was worth seeing the look of surprise on Julie's face. Now that she knew he was real, she would have to make a decision about him. There was something inside of him that wouldn't allow his sister not to like his alter ego. He knew it was probably petty, especially now, but it was still important.

His smile disappeared as Shiloh reached his point to await the meteor. He had arrived at his designated spot a few minutes early, so before he launched into space, he took a moment to let it sink in. Noticing Shiloh's hesitation, Mattis remained silent.

Shiloh looked down at a view only astronauts had ever seen.

So blue.

And so big.

The only other time he had been this high he had been so busy learning who he was and what he could do that somehow he never took the time to notice just how big everything seemed. Shiloh suddenly felt small and alone.

He turned his attention in the other direction. Without the thick haze of the atmosphere, he could see that the meteor was much larger than the one he had stopped over Thailand. Mattis provided detailed scans of the meteor, noting its construction and position and then highlighted the positions of the rest of the asteroids and meteors that would strike in the next few days.

Over a hundred lights appeared on his visor and Shiloh closed his eyes. There were just too many to think about.

A pit of fear stuck in his throat as he prepared to launch toward the massive hunk of rock.

"Let's do this," he said and started moving toward the meteor.

Then he felt it deep in his stomach; a tiny string of gravity still pulling at him. He was so used to feeling it while walking, at first he hadn't noticed it, but as he paid attention to the slight pull of his body's weight, he knew he wasn't moving.

"Mattis, what's happening? Am I out of gas?"

"You are not falling toward the planet, but you're not advancing either. You are hovering at the edge of the atmosphere," Mattis noted. "Almost precisely to the inch. Perhaps Witnesses are limited to terrestrial flight?"

"Now is not the time to find out!" Shiloh said.

Shiloh felt the mental muscle he used to fly. He flexed it as hard as he could, but could tell that he wasn't moving.

"Mattis, is there any way I can just stop flying and allow Earth to pass me, you know, so I can just kind of 'fall' out of the atmosphere?"

"Unlikely. If your powers are supernaturally limited, you will not be able to bypass those limitations without aid."

"That stinks! Plot the best course that will allow me to stop it."

Instantly, a glowing line appeared in his visor. It instantly corrected for Shiloh's inability to fly beyond the atmosphere. Shiloh turned and followed the line. Once he reached the circle Mattis placed in his view screen, he hovered in place.

With just three minutes remaining, Shiloh looked at the meteor again.

"*This is gonna hurt,*" he thought.

Shiloh closed his eyes for a moment. The coming days

would be very difficult even if they survived. He thought back to his ancestor Arter, wondering if he thought anything like this was ever possible. Shiloh wondered if he were watching somewhere and if he was, Shiloh hoped he was proud.

Dale Barkman had been the Communications Officer for Air Force One for twelve years. He knew the equipment in the President's plane better than anyone, but he was unable to trace this new feed. It was obviously from the same source that first informed them about the meteors and even the NSA couldn't trace that one. So when this new video feed appeared, the comm officer woke the President.

As a precaution, the President and Vice-President had been assigned to their respective planes. The Speaker of the House, assigned to an underground bunker, had pitched a fit that if the President and Vice President were going in their jets that she was going in her new private, taxpayer-funded jet, which she insisted everyone refer to as 'Air Force 3'. She made an angry call to the President, who was already in the air. The President calmed her long enough to order the Secret Service to fly her around. After she hung up, he instructed them to take her around a few hours and then stuff her back in the bunker if they had to.

It felt cowardly not only hiding from the meteor but hiding the fact that it was coming from the American people, but his advisors – who all insisted on being on the plane with him – were unanimous. It would invoke an unnecessary panic that would only increase suffering.

So the President, Vice President and apparently the Speaker of the House left in their planes to safeguard American democracy. If only he could believe there would be an America to return to.

The comm officer's call awoke him from his troubled

sleep. He sat on the side of the bed in his jogging clothes, fighting the urge to grab a cigarette. No smoking in the White House... to his dying day, he would believe that to be the single greatest mistake in his campaign.

After a press conference early in the campaign, he had snuck out a backstage door to grab a smoke, but as soon as he lit it, reporters looking to do the same thing walked in on him. After a few awkward seconds, the reporters grinned and lit up. For that one brief moment they were no longer candidate and reporters; they were fellow nicotine victims sharing in their daily afflictions.

One of the reporters had joked that the White House would have to buy ashtrays if he were elected and the then-candidate put on his best campaign voice and joked that though he was a smoker, the White House would remain smoke free to save the children and pets of the world from second, third and fourth hand smoke. The reporters laughed at his little joke and he hadn't thought anything about it until he saw the headlines the next day.

The reporters actually quoted what he said.

For the next week, American newspapers prominently featured stories about the candidate's deep commitment to keeping children and pets safe from the threat of the newly discovered 'third' and 'fourth hand smoke'. He was furious until his campaign manager pointed out that the media had managed to out him as a smoker in a sympathetic manner.

"His only flaw", an SNMBC commentator noted, wiping tears away from his puffy face, "And he still looks out for children and pets."

Television experts spent the next two weeks theorizing what the candidate was talking about, but everyone had a different take. The most popular theory was made by a scientist who believed that 'fourth hand smoke' was the visual sensation of seeing someone smoke, which furthered societal acceptance of smoking, so in that context, "fourth hand smoke" was more dangerous than all of the others combined because it was the root cause of first, second and third hand smoke.

It was almost enough to make a guy quit smoking for real. The President entered the monitoring room and popped in a stick of nicotine gum. The communications officer remained busy at his console, going over some hand written calculations.

He seemed surprised at his own conclusions.

"What do you have there, Captain Barkman?"

"Sir, approximately two minutes ago, Air Force One was sent a new video feed. I don't know how they hacked into our system, but you need to see this. It's a live orbit feed."

The President sat down and leaned toward the screen. The shot was erratic and amateurish; almost as if someone was holding a camcorder on his shoulder in the middle of space. But that wasn't possible. He was informed anytime a nation launched something into orbit and no manned missions were currently underway.

"There's also an audio feed attached, but there's not enough air to carry sound at that altitude."

"What have we learned so far?"

"Someone is in orbit when no nation on Earth has a current manned orbital mission. And this isn't an automated camera, either; take a look at this."

After rewinding the video several minutes, he stopped at one frame.

"See that?" he asked, pointing to the lower part of the screen.

The President leaned in and after he saw what Captain Barkman was pointing to, leaned in even closer.

"Is that a shoe?"

"Yes, sir. After I notified you of the signal, I aimed a few of our spy satellites in that direction. Let's see, I can bring them up... here."

Captain Barkman punched a few buttons on his control panel and three other monitors displayed the images of a man standing in the middle of the blackness of space.

"That's the owner of our shoe. I calculated that..."

"Hello?" A voice intruded from the video feed. "I don't have much time, so you need to listen," Shiloh said.

The video feed jerked toward the incoming meteor. It was large in the camera's lens and approaching fast.

"I can stop this thing. Well, I'm pretty sure I can. But there are a bunch of asteroids coming after this and I just want to make sure you guys are ready to throw everything you have in case I'm... not here."

"Where's this feed coming from?" The President asked.

"I'm, uh, I think I'm about four hundred miles above the Earth," Shiloh replied.

"You can hear me?" the President asked, surprised. There were no microphones in the monitoring room.

"Yeah, and you're not making me feel very confident right now."

"We sent two nuclear warheads at the meteor you're facing now. It didn't stop it."

"Well, it had to have sheared off a few tons. That's gotta help."

"Who is this and how am I able to hear you?"

"I'm the guy who stopped your crazy Congresswoman from killing all those people in San Francisco, remember?"

"The Windy City Angel?"

"Actually, if you're going to call me something, I'd rather be called The Witness. And as to how you can hear me, I have no idea. I'm still trying to figure all this out myself."

The President leaned in toward the best video shot of Shiloh he had. Without his brightly colored mantle, Shiloh would've been almost invisible against the black backdrop of space. The President jumped back when Shiloh waved toward the camera.

"If you don't think it's too big a violation of the Constitution, say a prayer for me, okay? I've got family down there, too, you know."

The President watched the monitors as the meteor approached.

"Good luck," the President said.

"I hope you meant to say Godspeed," Shiloh said.

Then the meteor hit.

The explosion blinded the cameras. Shiloh's feed was instantly lost. One high speed camera managed to get Shiloh and the meteor in the same frame, but the next few frames were filled with angry static and then nothing.

People on the ground felt the explosion, which produced a loud thunderclap that scattered across North America.

"What happened?" the President asked.

Captain Barkman put the head of NASA on the speaker phone. Together, they scanned through several monitors, playing back the video.

"Wormwood Three is shattered," the man said. "But our angel is gone. Repeat: Our angel is gone."

The President lowered his head.

"Assemble the press corps for an announcement at eight. It's time to let everyone know."

Alban Tor piously took his place on the platform behind the podium marked with the seal of the President of the United States. An army of reporters were packed in the White House Press Room, whispering to each other like anxious schoolgirls. Alban passed the time by rubbing his yellowed teeth on his shirt sleeve.

Hygiene wasn't one of Alban's priorities.

The President had personally asked him to speak to the nation. Unknown to the reporters before him, as soon as the cameras went live, Alban would be introduced as the judge, jury and executioner for every man, woman and child who lived on planet Earth.

Such was the power of Science and Alban was one of Science's High Priests. Hailed as the world's foremost authority on the solar system, Alban had actually only conducted two studies in his life, both of which were later denounced, but at the time sent shock waves through the scientific community. In over thirty years of study, he had always been careful to allow for his interviews to be safely taped and edited, furthering his claim of scientific authority.

If scientists could not save the Earth, then they reserved the power to pronounce its judgment. And Alban determined that they would do it without the mythological veils of deity that mankind had hidden behind for millennia.

Mankind, he had decided, would go out with open eyes.

Alban sneered as he thought about the headlines over the past few weeks. It all started months earlier with some nonsense about a flying man saving some children from a carjacking and then more recently, intervening in a hostage situation.

The stories caught his attention, but not because of their fantastic nature. He knew a government cover-up when he saw one and if something wasn't being covered up, it soon would. So Alban wasn't surprised when he heard about the asteroids.

It all made sense.

Though brutish in its logic, it was actually quite clever. The government had to create a hero to introduce the concept of asteroids without causing mass panic. As long as humanity had hope – regardless how outlandish the situation or slim the chances – they would cling to that hope just as they clung to their guns and their religion and nothing that was said or done could shake them loose from that last thread of hope.

Of course, the hero couldn't stop all of the asteroids, so he would have to conveniently die after stopping the first few, a tidy bookend to their fairy tale.

And since there was simply no way a government could cover up the vast destruction caused by an actual meteor, reason said there never was a meteor. Oh, he had seen the video of destruction from the so-called "falling pieces" of the meteor, but they had obviously been staged. A meteor would have created a large crater and a worldwide covering of dust, not large piles of rocky debris.

Alban sighed.

Would that he were naive enough to indulge a belief in mythical beings who could magically save the day. But today would prove that it was too late for even the government to continue the charade. He looked knowingly at a reporter in the front row, an elderly lady who had been a regular fixture in the White House press corps for almost five decades. One of the few reporters he corresponded with, he met with her before the conference, slipping her a piece of paper with the question he was not allowed to publicly ask.

The back doors opened and the President entered. His shoulders hung low and his walk was uncharacteristically shallow. The press cheered and as he approached the podium, he held his hands up to quiet them. It took a few moments for the applause to die down, but instead of the sly grin that he usually flashed reporters, the President looked up with tired, weary eyes.

"Ladies and gentlemen, as many of you know, Dr. Alban Tor is the world's greatest authority on the solar system. He will be making a statement, after which I will take questions. Dr. Tor?"

Alban stood and took a moment to look around at the faces, full of question and wonder. He cleared his throat and leaned forward.

"Today is a grave moment for the history of the planet Earth for today we learn the day that life on our planet will end. Over the past two weeks, the United Nations satellite project has identified and is tracking a number of objects on a collision course with the Earth and Moon."

Alban paused to let the moment set in. The deathly quiet of the room was punctured by the humbled voice of a reporter in the back.

"My God," she whispered.

"Five days from now, over one hundred astral bodies of varying sizes will intersect Earth's orbit. There is no hope of survival. Even if there was a possibility that the impact wouldn't destroy all life – and there is not - the Earth itself will be struck with enough force to push us out of orbit and perhaps even collapse into the sun's gravitational pull."

Alban sat down. The President returned to the podium

and held his hands out to belay questions.

"The United States government, in conjunction with the UN Security Council, has secretly been launching nuclear weapons in an attempt to circumvent the incoming threat, with no success, but contrary to Dr. Tor's assertion, we believe there is hope. Many of you have seen reports concerning the Windy City Angel. That man, who goes by the codename 'Witness', has already stopped several of the meteors."

The President motioned off camera and the view changed to a grainy video of a man standing in the blackness of space. It took a few seconds to notice that the video was being played back in slow motion. In frame after frame, there was just an image of the man and then suddenly in the space of one frame, it looked like the man was standing in the middle of a mountain.

The next frames were solid white, followed by nothing.

The video feed returned to the President, wiping the corners of his mouth in frustration.

"We have not heard from him since intercepting this meteor over the Atlantic."

The President paused as he considered his next words.

"Wherever he is, we... pray for his quick recovery. The first two asteroids will strike the planet within the next forty-eight hours. Three days later, a wave of over one hundred asteroids will pummel..."

The reporters jumped to their feet yelling questions and for the first time in his political career, the President had to fight them for control. After a minute of holding his hands up, the press subsided.

"We are urging everyone to gather potable water and find a place to secure your family as best you can."

The President's head lowered and a wave of reporters' hands flew up.

In their home, the Wagners sat on their couch, numbly watching the Presidential press conference. Despite the fact that Mattis had already told them the asteroids were coming, it hadn't actually sunk in until they saw the President announce it.

Originally, George was going to send Julie to her room, but decided that she was old enough to know what was coming. When they returned from All-Mart, Tina was sent to her room with a cheese pizza and bubblegum flavored cola. Lillian looked over at Julie as the press conference droned on, noticing tears running down her face.

"Jules, no matter what happens, we're together."

"Where's Shiloh?"

Lillian looked at her husband with grief in her eyes.

"I don't know, baby. We've left messages on his cell."

"He needs to come home. What if something happened to him?"

Julie collapsed into her mother's arms.

"John Cooper, NCC," a voice blared above the other reporters. "Is there a chance Dr. Tor is wrong? His earlier studies on global cooling were found to be wrong just before he started warning us about global warming."

Dr. Tor fumed, but kept his peace. Most people had forgotten that thirty years earlier he was the head of a movement that warned of global cooling which would make the Earth uninhabitable for humans within the next century. One reporter compared his speeches then and now and found that he was using the exact same language to predict that global warming would make the Earth uninhabitable within the next century. Dr. Alban protested to the paper and the reporter was fired.

"Our own scientists have corroborated his findings," The President said. "In fact, that is why you've been experiencing satellite and internet interference these past few days. We censored any mention of the incoming threat to avoid public panic."

"Sean Colmes, Newsfox," another voice said. "Has any effort been made to see if the Witness survived the impact of the last meteor? If so, have you made any attempts to contact him?"

"Our satellites followed the blast after the Witness intercepted the meteor, but we haven't heard anything from him since that time. We are hopeful that he survived."

"Mr. President," a smarmy old voice from the front row called out as a thinly veined arm craned up to catch his attention. Alban smiled as his card was about to be played.

"Isn't it true that this 'Witness' persona was just manufactured to give false hope that he will appear at the last minute to save us all? Surely you can't expect us to believe it's a coincidence that a superman happened to appear just before our world is about to be destroyed by asteroids, do you?"

The question caught the President off-guard. Ellen Jefferson normally only attacked the opposing party's chief executives.

"Ellen, if that were so, I would have concocted a hundred supermen. The fact is that this individual is real, but aside from his activities in Chicago and San Francisco, we only know that he displays superhuman abilities. Because of that, we are optimistic that he survived his impact with the meteor as he obviously did the first meteor and will continue to believe so unless we find out differently. Last question."

"Bill Wheat, AKFN. What are you doing at this point?"

"This morning, the United States, in conjunction with Israel, the United Kingdom, Russia, China, Japan and India began launching every space vehicle in our fleets. Our top astronauts will travel outside the influence of the asteroids' destructive path, carrying samples of technology as well as every historical and medical journal available. Their mission will be to preserve a record of who we are for any future generations who may survive or other life forms who come our way."

The reporters stood awaiting the President's next words. When he spoke, he turned away from his ever present teleprompters to look directly into the camera.

"People of the United States of America and of the planet Earth: If it's our time to go, then there's nothing I can say or do to change that. But if life continues on this planet, things will not be the same as they have been. Conditions will most likely be barbaric, hostile and even inhumane. Look out for each other. The human race is at stake. God bless the planet Earth."

The President turned away and the reporters remained silent behind him. After the President left, the cameras remained on the closed door and news anchors the world over tried to instruct their citizens how to best prepare for the final wave of asteroids. A few blamed the asteroids on the previous administration's policies.

The downtown warehouse was old and incredibly large. Originally built for experimental weapon manufacturing in World War II, it sat vacant on the Joliet, Illinois landscape except for annual visits from a maintenance crew. No one knew who owned the building. The property taxes were paid from a private trust fund. Each year it sat, an empty tax burden, just waiting for the annual return of the maintenance crew.

Until last year.

At first, everyone thought the maintenance crew was returning for their upkeep, but then large trucks began arriving and heavy equipment was carried in. For the next week, crates were unloaded day in and day out - heavy crates stamped with a weird foreign language.

Then the trucks stopped coming and smoke started belching from the stacks for the first time since the forties. That's when the rumors began. Some said that Joliet had been chosen as an emergency backup to Ft. Knox in case of a terrorist attack. Others thought the warehouse was housing secret alien technology and the smoke stacks were being operated to cover its true nature.

But, as with most things, the truth was much simpler.

The trucks were bringing in tons of raw Norse iron ore and the equipment necessary to purify it. Huge smelters had been installed to process the metal and over the past year the plant had processed almost eight hundred pounds of pure ore, slow even by ancient standards, but the men had been paid to ensure the highest quality iron possible.

The smoke had again become a regular part of the Joliet

landscape, so no one was even talking about it when the trucks came again this year. There were only two and this time when the trucks came, the smoke stopped.

Leif lay in darkness, entombed in the armor, numbly trying to stay sane. Something was wrong. He never slept or ate or even drank and yet he was still alive. He remained in the exact same state he had been when they had sealed him in; hungry, thirsty and tired.

He couldn't eat.

He couldn't drink.

He couldn't even sleep.

Several times his mind began wandering into what he thought would be the welcoming arms of insanity, but then something would snap him back to his weary existence. Whatever was keeping him alive was keeping him just on this side of sanity, but Leif could feel his spirit drowning in its own mortality.

His first few days had been spent crying in a helpless state. His uncle had never again spoken to Leif, even though he saw him several times. After a while, his mind became incredibly focused, assessing the situation and that's when the anger came. The next time he was given control over the armor, he would kill Andris Laima, without question or hesitation.

He had made himself familiar with the suit's internal operations. He couldn't move. His uncle had disabled any kind of control when the suit was inactive, but Leif had still managed to decipher the suit's controls. He was a novice with computers, but the intuitive interface had been designed to be simple enough for a moron to operate. And he had plenty of time to learn how the controls were mapped out.

Several of the suit's functions were disabled, but he found the access port for each of the battle functions, including self-destruct. Before he was placed in the suit, nothing would have made Leif think of taking his own life, but this wasn't life. The next time his armor was powered up for testing, Leif would tear the organs from his uncle's living chest and then trigger the self-destruct mechanism built into the armor and end this facade.

He had been placed inside a crate a week earlier and, through the onboard GPS, was able to track where he was at any given moment. Even though the suit had not been charged since the séance that trapped him inside, the suit's power readout always showed 132% of capacity. It made things very warm in the armor, even more since its internal cooling had been disabled, but it didn't matter. Leif dreamed of the blessing of mere discomfort.

He was uncrated in the warehouse and placed on a stone altar like the one in his uncle's castle. If circumstances were different, Leif would be amazed at the technology inherent in the armor. But during the trip over, he accessed a part of the database that at one point had been restricted. After opening the file, he saw that the suit was scheduled for a demonstration this very night in a city named Joliet. At the thought of being free in any capacity, he smiled for the first time since entering the suit. GPS confirmed it was nearly night and he was in Joliet, Illinois. That's all he needed to know.

Andris Laima would die - tonight - in Joliet, Illinois.

Julie Wagner was tired, but although it was after midnight, she couldn't sleep. The asteroid was less than twenty-four hours away.

How could she sleep?

As a silly precaution, she opened her curtains. Her upstairs bedroom had a clear view of the eastern sky and if something was going to kill her, she wanted to see it coming. Julie began thinking about her life and how unfair it was for this to happen when she was only seventeen. She always made fun of her mom and dad for being born thirty years earlier, but now she was envious of them and even more so of her grandparents. They got to live their lives - full lives - but she'd never get the chance to go to college or fall in love or get married.

In the night time silence, Julie heard muffled crying from the room next door. She softly paced into Tina's room.

"Hey, what's wrong?" she asked her sister.

Tina's face peeked out from the small jumble of covers.

"We're going to die," she whispered.

"Baby, no one's going to die," Julie lied.

"The news said the rocks are going to kill everyone. People were crying."

Tina erupted from beneath the blankets and grabbed Julie. No matter how bad she had it, Julie couldn't imagine what it would be to take the news at nine. She held Tina tight, rocking her in her arms, just like she did when Tina was born. It had been a long time since she felt this close to her baby sister. For the first two years of Tina's life,

Julie almost thought of herself as Tina's second mom. She was glad she was told to take Tina out. Besides, she got to see her angel.

That's right, and Julie realized that she did, too. She had seen the Witness with her own eyes and a tiny spark of hope began to crystallize inside her own heart.

He was real.

And if he was real, then there was still hope.

"Tina, do you remember the angel we saw today?"

"They say he died, too!"

"Tina Wagner, angels can't die! Do you believe he's an angel?"

"Yes," she whimpered.

"Then he won't rest until every rock in the sky is broken into a million pieces and we're all safe."

"Promise?"

"I don't have to promise, you know it's true."

It took ten minutes of consoling before Tina fell asleep. Julie watched her for a few minutes longer to make sure she was sound asleep and eased her arm out from beneath Tina until the pillow cradled her sister's head.

Before she could return to her room, a large boom filled the house, shaking the entire foundation.

It was too soon to be a meteor, but something large had hit the house. Tiptoeing down the stairs, she saw her father come out of his bedroom with his pistol. He placed a finger over his lips and motioned for her to return to her room.

Normally, Julie would have been too scared not to obey, but her life was going to end in hours anyway. She watched her father walk toward the back porch and quietly followed behind him. They had all trained with her dad's pistol, but she never imagined him ever having to use it.

George Wagner had been sleeping when he was jolted

out of his sleep by the impact. It felt like a truck had struck the house. He grabbed his pistol and motioned for his wife to stay in bed. After making sure it was loaded, George removed the safety and eased out of his bedroom as silently as he could.

Movement.

To his right.

The upstairs hall light was just bright enough for him to see Julie coming down the stairs and he lowered his pistol. His heart was racing fast.

If only Shiloh were here.

He motioned for Julie to return to her room and then silently moved toward the back of the house. A street light spilled into his backyard, so it was well lit enough for him to peer through the kitchen curtains.

The backyard was a scene of total devastation. Only a small crater and a few branches existed where the tree used to be. The yard itself was a massive pile of dirt and swing set parts.

George cautiously opened the back door and stepped outside. There was no breeze or sound of any kind other than a slow hiss emanating from the crater. Whatever had crashed had caused quite a mess. George climbed over the first small piles of dirt to peer inside, pistol first.

Then he tripped and fell inside.

"Dad!" Julie screamed as she ran out the back door. She raced to the crater, climbing over the mound. She was shocked when she looked inside the crater because she didn't see one person.

She saw two.

Her father helped the other person to their feet, but their heads barely cleared ground level. That's when Julie noticed who the other person was. He had a helmet and was wearing a cape.

It was the Witness!

"Oh my God! Let me help!" she cried out, stretching her arm down as far as she could. The man in the helmet stumbled for a moment and ignored her arm, slowly levitating them both out of the crater.

And then he collapsed.

Multiple sirens started wailing in the distance and George stood to his feet in a panic as he realized an army of emergency vehicles was headed his way. The neighbors' lights were turning on. No doubt his friend and closest neighbor Pete Gallagher would be over in moments. Pete was a good neighbor, but this wasn't the time.

They had to get Shiloh inside before someone saw him.

"Quick, grab an arm!" George said, and Julie put her head under his left arm while her father grabbed his right arm. Julie expected to strain, but the man was lighter than she had imagined, well under two hundred pounds. And he wasn't as tall as he seemed earlier on the road.

They carried him into the house and carefully laid him on the couch. Lillian came out of her bedroom and took one look at the caped man.

"Shiloh!" she cried and ran over to him. She tried to pull his helmet off, but it wouldn't budge.

"That's Shiloh?" Julie asked, bewildered.

"He said he'll be alright," George said.

"He looks horrible!"

Julie went to the kitchen and returned with wet towels and handed them to her mother. She tore them in strips and began cleaning the thick soot and blood from his clothes.

A soft hiss came from his helmet and Shiloh pulled it off. He blinked his eyes in pain.

"I'll be okay...just need a shower and some sleep. I've got to stop the first real big one tomorrow."

Shiloh sat up on the couch and tried to stand, but his

knee bent at an odd angle and he fell back down.

"Maybe you could help me upstairs," he admitted.

A desperate knock came at the front door. It was Pete, in his house robe and sneakers, carrying a rifle.

"George!" he yelled through the front door. "Everyone okay?"

Pete continued knocking loudly. He leaned nervously into the door window, scraping his large glasses against the pane.

"Julie, we'll talk later," George said.

"Is that why you couldn't tell me where Shiloh was?"

"Help your mom get him to his room."

George headed to the front door and faked fumbling with the lock as Shiloh's mother and sister helped him hobble up the stairs. Pete almost burst through the door when it opened.

"What the heck happened?"

"Something hit in the backyard. I think it was a small meteor or something."

"I tried to get through the back gate, but it's mangled!"

"The back yard is all tore up. Whatever it was, it took out the tree and Tina's swing set."

"Let's go," Pete said, inviting himself inside.

George led Pete out the back.

Julie opened Shiloh's door and they led him inside. Shiloh tossed his helmet to the floor and collapsed on his bed.

"How long have you guys known?" Julie asked.

"Honey, not now," her mother said.

"S'okay," Shiloh whispered. "Just please stop yelling."

"He needs rest," Shiloh's mother said, pulling Julie away.

They left the room for a long talk, Shiloh imagined.

In the room next to Shiloh's, Tina remained hidden under her covers, afraid of the noise and sirens and smoke and most of all that her parents were afraid of the rocks in the sky that were coming to kill them all.

"Where's my angel, God?" she asked, her tiny voice cracking.

Shiloh lay on his bed looking in the direction of his little sister's room wondering the same thing.

Mosh entered Shiloh's ship, but wasn't allowed past the vestibule. Sensors scanned his body as the hatch shut behind him.

"What's wrong? I thought we trusted each other."

"This is standard boarding procedure for all royal vessels," Mattis replied.

Mosh huffed as he waited. The scans finished and the interior doors opened. The entrance lit as he stepped through it. As he walked down the hall, Mosh noted that all the doors had been closed except the one he was instructed to enter.

The hold was small, barely as large as the smaller bays in his ship. As Mosh looked around, he realized he had never seen such detail in a ship. Even the wall brackets were hand crafted. It was a shame that a ship this fine had to be destroyed.

"There's not enough conduits available," Mosh noted. "Do you have any more?"

"I have already calculated the necessary amount of modules. Any remaining conduit modules will be fitted to the panels in the personnel quarters aft of the hold. Spares are available in the cargo hold."

It took all afternoon for Mosh to hook up the modules and even though Mattis configured them, he still wondered if compatibility really would match his old ship.

"How are you coming along with my Earth identity?" Mosh asked.

"Everything is ready. As soon as the planet is secure,

you will be introduced to your new life. Two large homes and transportation have already been purchased."

Mosh grabbed one of the thicker power cables and yanked. It was barely long enough to reach the next module. The machine had indeed calculated down to the inch what was needed, but it didn't make his job any easier.

"So, who am I going to be?" he grunted.

"Peter Mantle, the only living descendant of James Mantle, the oil tycoon. Photos have been manipulated and an identity trail has been established, leading back to your fictional birth thirty-five years ago."

Mosh turned the ratchet, sealing the line and then hooked up the gravimeter to test the connection. Flow was good and capacity was better than he had hoped.

"Thirty-five? Right, years are different here."

"The only things I am unable to compensate for are the things you will quickly notice; the lighter atmosphere will mean that you tire more easily; your diet will have to be managed and you will have to take care that you are not exposed to the sun for extended periods of time."

"Sounds like paradise."

"You will enjoy far better living conditions than you experienced on Ehrets."

Mosh finished his adjustments, wiped his brow and allowed himself a smile as he accessed the last panel. Everything checked go.

"I didn't think I'd ever say this, but thanks, machine."

"You are welcome."

"Tell the kid that I'm gonna test the system one more time and then we're ready to go. The rest is up to him."

Shiloh awoke to the sound of his alarm clock. He didn't remember setting it, but it's a good thing he did. He was due to leave for the asteroid in less than fifteen minutes. Shiloh slowly sat up on the edge of his bed, trying to ignore the pain still housed deep in his bones.

He managed to sit up without falling over and leaned his head forward. Ever since he first learned about the asteroids, Shiloh had been frantically praying for the power of the Witness Imperium to be given to him early so that he would have the power needed to stop the coming asteroids, but he could tell without moving that he retained the power of the Witness Regent.

And he knew that power wasn't enough.

There was no way he could survive another impact like that and Mattis had said that the asteroid was magnitudes larger than the meteors he had stopped.

A knock on his door preceded the soft voice of his mother.

"Shay?"

"Still here, Mom."

Lillian Wagner let herself into her son's room. She saw Shiloh leaning his head down in prayer, something she hadn't seen him do in a long time.

"Did you get any answers?"

"I don't think God listens to me."

"Don't say that!"

"The asteroids are too big, Mom. They move too fast for me to do anything except get in the way. I don't think I can stop it."

Shiloh stood and picked up his helmet. Before he could put it on, Lillian hugged him.

"You don't have to go," she said. "You've already done your part."

But her words only firmed his resolve. Shiloh returned the hug.

"Yeah, I do, but thanks" he said, breaking contact and putting his helmet on.

His mom stared at him as he stood by the window.

"I love you, Mom. You and Dad say a prayer for me, okay?"

And before his Mom could reach him to hug him again, Shiloh leapt out the window and climbed into the sky.

He lifted high into the atmosphere, leaving his parents, his home and his concerns, hovering at ninety thousand feet. The night would assist him in seeing the asteroid. He groaned as a wave of pain racked through his body.

"What do I have to do?" he asked Mattis.

"Our ships are ready for the following groups of asteroids," Mattis said, and then noting Shiloh's pain and disposition tried to calm him.

"Just think of this asteroid and nothing more."

Mattis lit up a display showing a target area for Shiloh to travel to. Shiloh headed in the direction of the blip in time to see the first asteroid with his naked eyes.

It was the largest thing he had ever seen in his life.

"How close is it?"

"It will penetrate the atmosphere in four minutes."

Shiloh took a second and looked down. He was hovering over the Atlantic Ocean, east of Massachusetts. As he looked around, Mattis targeted individual satellites and even debris from other space missions.

Looking at the incoming asteroid was a reality check.

"Mattis, can I do this?"

"The actions of Witnesses Imperium have been cataloged over the centuries and based on those accounts, a Witness Imperium would be able to stop an asteroid, but you are just a Regent and there is very little historical detail of the limitations of Witnesses Regent."

"But you think I can, right?"

Mattis was in conflict; to protect the Regent, it had to place his life in jeopardy. It was a matter of simple logic. The Regent couldn't survive without a planet. Everything had been calculated down to the last erg of power needed to divert all the asteroids, but Mattis secretly knew it still wouldn't be enough. It had noted a large asteroid in the last wave that would be outside the effect of their makeshift gravimetric well and it wouldn't tell Shiloh – or anyone else – about it. After all was said and done, the last and largest of the asteroids would still strike the Earth.

But it bought them time and Mattis needed time to devise a plan to stop the last asteroid. Mattis couldn't let Shiloh know. His attention had to remain focused on this asteroid and then the next one. Mattis was gambling that Shiloh's divine protection from kinetic damage would protect him from the twin strikes, but it had left the realm of possible, operating solely in the realm of the theoretical, as it did whenever it considered the Witnesses.

"My opinion is irrelevant. Your powers operate outside the laws of physics."

"I'm as ready as I can be," Shiloh said, thinking of his parents and then out of nowhere, Shiloh thought of his father Eythan.

What would he do in this situation?

"Mattis, do you have any video of my dad...Eythan?"

"Yes, but is this the time?"

"Play it."

Mattis moved the live view of the asteroid to the upper

right section of Shiloh's view. The center panel was filled with a too perfect scene of Eythan and Shiloh sitting on the platform in the Court of Reconciliation. Eythan was all but smiling. The scene was a frozen moment of content and peace not just between a King and a Prince, but a father and his son.

Shiloh could tell that something was troubling his father, but a stubborn glint in his eye refused to give it place. He looked at his father's intricately woven beard and subconsciously scratched his naked chin. His father looked so powerful – so strong – occupying the throne as if he were born there.

Shiloh still couldn't believe he was dead.

Then, Shiloh couldn't help but notice how frightened his younger self seemed...how fragile and small he looked in the large throne to his father's right. Shiloh saw himself noticeably tense as his eyes fixed on something off-screen.

"Why did I jump like that?"

Mattis changed the view to the doorway. The doors opened and the guards stepped back as Gerah Maugaine entered the chamber. His walk was that of a man who was not to be stopped, his every step a personal declaration of power.

Shiloh involuntarily tensed as Gerah glanced directly at the camera. His glare remained directed at the camera as he marched toward the throne.

"That is General Gerah Maugaine, the man in charge of the war against your brother Grayden. It is odd that he is visible. Normally, the General didn't allow his image to be electronically captured."

"Why am I afraid of him?"

"Many people were afraid of him. His presence on the Council was extremely controversial. General Maugaine's actions constantly placed him outside and some said above the Law."

"No, I mean I'm afraid just looking at him now. It's like he can see me through the video."

"That is impossible."

"Well, you know me and 'impossible'. I can't explain it, but he's looking at me!"

"General Maugaine was reported to have supernatural powers akin to and perhaps greater than the Witnesses, but remote viewing was not one of them."

Regardless, the feeling was there; the same feeling Mosh talked about earlier.

Judgment.

"He's wondering if I'm going to turn out like my brother."

The thought of his elder brother brought a flash of anger. If Grayden hadn't rebelled, his father would be alive and Shiloh would be safe on Ehrets... and, the thought completed itself, everyone on Earth would be dead. His Mom, his Dad.

Everyone.

Shiloh looked at the asteroid as it grew in size and the reality of what he was doing occurred to him. Tears welled in his eyes as he realized that there was no turning back. But he also knew that if anyone below had a chance of survival, he had to stand his ground.

"Mattis, I don't want to die," he said, his voice cracking.

"Regent, the things you can do are a direct violation of everything I know to be a fact, but one thing is clear to me: you will not die. For all of the small reasons you wish to see as the basis of your existence, for every bank robbery and mugging you seek to tie your fate to, it is this threat that realizes your Calling. Your God has brought you to this time and place for a reason. You must have faith that He will not allow your death until your mission is done."

Shiloh stared at the asteroid.

"I will not fail," he whispered and he felt the history of a dozen Witnesses standing with him. Each generation had faced death in the realization of their missions. Some lived and some died, but that's what set apart the House of Arter from the House of Samson.

The Sons of Arter completed their mission or they died trying.

And that's when his fear disappeared into the freedom of purpose; the realization of who he was and what he was supposed to do and in that moment, death was no longer a threat.

Whatever was going to happen, this asteroid would not pass Shiloh Wagner.

Shiloh pulled back lower into the atmosphere. Sensing what he was doing, Mattis began a countdown to atmosphere penetration.

Fifteen seconds.

Shiloh looked one last time at Gerah's accusatory stare.

"I'm not my brother," Shiloh whispered and mentally wiped the image from his view screen.

Seconds before the asteroid reached the edge of the atmosphere, Shiloh launched toward it as fast as he could.

The impact resulted in the largest displacement of energy ever recorded on the planet Earth. Shiloh was instantly battered unconscious as the shell of the asteroid took the brunt of the discharge, shattering into a million billion pieces. Wave after wave of kinetic energy dissipated and the asteroid shattered into multi-ton shards as Shiloh's body tore through to the mile-wide iron core.

The asteroid surrendered the remainder of its momentum as eighty trillion megatons of kinetic energy disappeared. The shards which had broken off exploded into smaller pieces because of the instantaneous change of speed. The largest remaining pieces impacted off the coast of Massachusetts, triggering massive, but localized waves.

Shiloh was blown back by the aftershocks, falling toward the Atlantic Ocean. Mattis amplified a signal directly into his brain, but Shiloh barely reached consciousness. He felt the pain of a million hammers under his skin and bones as the remaining kinetic damage transferred from his body. His thoughts were murky as he strained to remember where he was and what he was doing, though he knew it was something important.

"Regent, you need to stop your fall!" Mattis yelled, but Shiloh slipped back into unconsciousness.

Mattis engaged its Control Program.

The core programming that Mattis had placed inside almost every processor on Earth years earlier gave it direct access and control of every piece of electronics in a three hundred mile radius. Mattis was able to follow and project the destruction that would be caused by the multiple impacts of the remaining pieces of asteroid. The final death toll would be in the thousands, but the Regent's actions had saved the planet.

Mattis calculated the rate of Shiloh's descent. In six minutes he would sink into the Atlantic Ocean. It would be better for the Regent to crash on a ship or plane than drown, even if that meant further injuring him.

Mattis reached out and took control of every airplane and ship within the projected impact zone. They instantly abandoned their mortal captains' orders to obey Mattis' electronic commands. Every vessel within Mattis' range changed course to converge on the same spot. The crews panicked as the engines revved up past all safety protocols, and then again when they saw that their ships were on a high speed collision course with each other, but there was nothing any of them could do.

The ships were almost at their destinations when Shiloh snapped awake. Fully conscious, he was surprised to be alive. His body was a mass of battered cells, past the point of numbness. His flesh was clammy and gray and lifeless.

It felt like he was wearing someone else's body.

But Shiloh felt something more powerful than his pain: a compulsion to go; to be somewhere; frantic and stronger than even the natural urge to breathe. Shiloh followed the compulsion west, but it didn't go away.

He couldn't explain it. It was as if history said that at that given moment, he was to be at a given location and he was panicking that he wouldn't be there in time.

"Regent, are you well?"

"No," Shiloh's jaws ached. "Must... go!"

"You are headed west. I am monitoring all police bands west of Cleveland, but am unable to find anything out of the ordinary. You must try to resist this urge. The next asteroid arrives in less than eight hours and you need the time to heal."

Shiloh tore through the skies of Ohio, as fast as Mattis said he could fly, passing Indiana in minutes. When he reached Joliet, Illinois, he turned north and followed the Des Plaines River.

Then it made no difference that it made no sense.

Something warned Shiloh as surely as if someone were tapping him on the shoulder and pointing in a direction. Shiloh turned to look to see where the danger was coming from.

Once he looked in the right direction, it was easy to see.

A local warehouse was covered by large clouds. The thunderhead was broiling like water on a stove, churning its black mass through the building.

"Weird...cloud," Shiloh said, pointing at the warehouse.

"I don't detect any clouds in the direction you are looking."

Shiloh headed toward the warehouse and Mattis began seeking all available information about the building. Sold through a number of fronts, the tracks ended in Eastern Europe where the electronic trail turned into an undocumented paper trail. Though it couldn't determine the owner's identity, Mattis did notice something about some of its most recent occupants. A local coven had met there several times over the past few months, even advertising on their website, jolietwicca.com.

"Be careful, Regent; this building is a worship site for the Kawshaf."

"Don't know... that word," Shiloh said, straining his partially restored memory of his home world Ehrets.

"Witches."

"For real?"

"This particular mawsoreth – you would say coven - is not one of the many amateur groups that I have been monitoring. This coven has been involved with several dangerous rituals over the past few years. It is no doubt unholY grounD."

"Mystical cloud?" Shiloh asked, fighting the pain in his jaws to form even simple words.

Mattis didn't have time to explain.

Small arcs of electricity flowed around the cloud and a cobalt knife stabbed into the Joliet sky. Though several hundred yards away, Shiloh instinctively covered his eyes. The roar of the explosion was deafening, though people walking around the structure continued moving as if nothing had happened.

Shiloh didn't see the lightning branching out of the

cloud or have time to react to it. The bolt lanced from cloud to cloud and then bent with an arcane twist, drawn to Shiloh. It pounded him and he fell – paralyzed -- to the ground below.

Leif had been lying dormant on the stone altar for hours. His only direct view was of the domed window above him. The prism he had retrieved was somehow floating above him, but he wasn't paying it any attention. The suit was partially powered and Leif was already scanning the warehouse. There were fourteen people in the immediate vicinity. He recognized the voices of the men who had trapped him in the armor. They had been standing around and chanting for the past few minutes. But before he was able to locate his uncle, the dome above him shattered.

As he looked through his visor to detect the cause, he caught a glimpse of something large and black. Leif tried to sit up to get off the slab, but couldn't move. He strained uselessly within his armored tomb.

And then the prism flashed brightly above him.

A sound accompanied the light, penetrating the seals of his armor. A melodic thunder - deep and dark - surrounded him like an aural shroud. Leif's back teeth rattled with the sound and the bones in his chest vibrated to the point he could feel the edges of each of his ribs with each note.

Leif screamed, but no sound came from his mouth, only the constant thrumming of the unearthly sound penetrating his skull as the light above him grew brighter and brighter. As the blazing fog settled into a thin white veil of air, Leif saw a warrior hovering above him, encased in a dome of some kind. Its face had all the elements of a human face, but it was not human.

The warrior looked at Leif with an ancient hatred as if

he had personally hated Leif for thousands of years.

Then Leif felt it...the link between him, the demon warrior and the armor, a twisted triangular vacuum drawing each other together. Though sealed in the armor, he could hear – he could feel - the demon's wail.

It was coming for him.

After all of this testing were they finally going to kill him? All thoughts of hunger and thirst disappeared in a fog of terror as the demon penetrated the armor, and they faced each other. The demon stared directly into Leif's eyes and for a moment, Leif thought he was seeing through the demon's eyes, because he was looking at himself.

Scared and shaking, he felt the full fury of the demon as it filled his body and the suit. The armor warped with the influx of energy as the demon fought to escape.

Leif felt an itch in his chest which quickly became a stabbing pain. The demon entered into his body and the prism erupted, fusing the three: demon, man and armor into a single being manifest on three levels; spirit, flesh and machine.

A Tri-Fest.

The attempt to fuse the spiritual energy into a mechanical and flesh union seared the prisM, but it held. The eldritch power coursed through the cobalt crystal like a river until it hit a chink. The small crack Leif had caused had slightly damaged the bottom character at one of the corners. Through that crack, energy began to seep and more energy began to flow, multiplying itself over and over.

The resultant explosion filled not just the warehouse, but most of the surrounding city block and splinters of energy stabbed out like lightning in all directions, both locally and afar, but the main bolt shot straight up, higher and higher, drawn toward a like force, finally bouncing off the atmosphere, branching back down over the eastern horizon.

Bolt after bolt erupted from the explosion until its eldritch energy had been spent. Then everything became quiet inside the warehouse.

Except for the grating sound of metal on stone as the suit of armor pulled itself from the altar and stood to its feet.

The Seven dwelt invisibly above the world of man, quietly watching the nations pass beneath their collective gaze. The Malak were the first angels to give their lives in defense of man in Helel's War. As such, they were deemed the guardian angels of mankind and after they were raised were given the rare freedom to intercede in the affairs of man.

Many successes and failures followed over the centuries as they found their power and influence blunted by man's stubborn resistance to following the higher path. Most of the Seven had given up hope by the time Samson was born, but their interest was sparked when Gabriel visited them, explaining that God had promised a son to a woman who could not conceive.

"The Promised One?" The faces of the Seven lit up at the possibility.

"No," Gabriel replied. "But this man will be unlike any other mortal ever born. He will be given power to change the course of this world."

"What of Ehrets? And the promised balance of worlds?"

"The balance shall remain intact. A man of like countenance shall be granted the same gift on Ehrets."

"Our only regret is that we are not able to interact with the humans of Ehrets. How does their world fair?"

"They made different choices and their world benefits from those choices."

"Would that this world would have been spared their suffering."

"They were given the same choices. The worlds operate on such strict physical laws that, until man accepts his place in it, he will fail."

"They subconsciously hearken to their spiritual side and then become confused when things don't work as they plan," One of the Seven noted. "Dual natures in one body. It must be frightening."

Gabriel smiled as he explained.

"This one shall be given access to spiritual powers to which mankind has been previously restricted."

The Seven then withdrew from the affairs of mankind to silently observe Samson's fate. Nothing in his childhood was out of the ordinary and the Seven began to wonder why their attention had been directed to this one man. Though a bit taller than his fellows, Samson lacked the sheer body volume that most Jewish men had developed over a lifetime of hard work.

Because of the special circumstances surrounding his birth, his father Manoah made sure that Samson lived a privileged life. Besides his restrictions from wine, cutting his hair and touching dead things, Samson was allowed to do whatever he wished. This caused great friction between him and the other boys in the village and Samson grew up an arrogant loner.

That all changed during a trip to Timnah. His parents agreed to take him to see a Philistine woman whom he desired to marry. They left a day before Samson to make preparations.

On the day he left, Samson was daydreaming about his wife to be, not paying attention to his surroundings. Most young men would have stayed on the beaten path, but Samson wandered around. He didn't notice the lion pacing him at a distance.

The Malak's first reaction was to stop the lion and save

Samson, but something stayed their hand. Samson didn't notice the lion until it had pounced and then it was too late.

The Malak expected to see Samson torn into pieces as the lion's next meal. But things changed after the lion knocked Samson to the ground. Physical eyes would have seen nothing different from one moment to the next, but the Malak stood back in awe as a wave of power spiritually flooded Samson's body.

The lion's sharp claws tried to sink into his flesh to better hold its prey, but they merely slid off his unprotected skin. Samson held the lion back and with a slightly confused, but growing confidence, fought back. It was over the instant Samson grabbed the beast's jaws. He tore them apart as easily as if he had been fighting a small cat.

The Malak then closely followed Samson's exploits. Though his motivations were always self-serving, they saw the hand of God on Samson's life, sparking their hope in the potential of man.

It only served to double their disillusion when Samson failed.

After his death and the failure of his promise, the Seven resigned their call, abandoning the world of man. They removed themselves to the edge of the atmosphere where they awaited a greater Call in the Last Days.

Though many events had occurred in the last three thousand years that they normally would have prevented, they stood their ground. Pain and tears and misery flooded the world of men and though they shared in the suffering of each pain and every death, they remained at their stations.

As America passed beneath each angel, they found their attention drawn to it...murder and rape and thievery and lies and blasphemy.

Just another night in America.

Then their vision blurred as a spiritual wave erupted in

the heart of the country. Like an ethereal earthquake, the vibrations surged, growing stronger and stronger until they covered the entire globe.

Then it happened.

An explosion of supernatural power stabbed into the night skies, spiritually polluting the atmosphere with its stench. Its shock waves covered the Earth, blocking the vision of the Malak.

The Warriors strained, but were unable to see through the spiritual mud. Whatever was occurring was outside their duty to stop.

The Warriors could only grab their swords tightly, close their eyes and await the Call.

The world of Shiloh's birth had changed drastically in the decade since he had last been there. Politically, spiritually and socially, Ehrets was simply a different world. Throne City, once the center of political and social activity of all Arterra, stood quiet except for the soldiers that patrolled its newly reconstructed gates.

The Temple of Jusinan was the single remnant of Ehret's former glory. Its golden towers and elaborate parapets could still be seen from miles away. The people who had lost contact with the throne had grown closer to the altar and they came by the millions each year to offer sacrifice, but it wasn't the same. The man responsible for the changes hadn't really wanted them.

Not like this.

After taking the throne, he tried to tell the people his side of the story; that he was only fighting for his rightful inheritance, stolen from him as the result of a foolish promise made by his father. As such, he only sought to retrieve what was rightfully his and nothing more. Since he didn't have the power to directly contest the throne, he had to find something that did.

At one time he was more of a practical man than religious, but after obtaining the prisM, Grayden had come to know the world of the supernatural firsthand. That's when everything began to change; the murder of his father and the exile of his younger brother Shiloh, who had been made heir apparent during Grayden's exile.

He forced the Council into recognizing him as Witness Imperium, but without the mantle, the small piece of ivory cloth that had been handed down to every Witness since Arter himself, their words of submission rang hollow.

What Grayden hadn't counted on was the price he had to pay when he took possession of the prisM...or rather, when it had taken possession of him. He had tried many times to get rid of it after assuming the throne, but he might as well have tried to get rid of his fingers.

And the voices...

Some of the spirits of those slaughtered by the prisM resided inside the crystal and as long as Grayden remained planet-side, their maddening curses almost drove him insane. Reluctantly, he moved his operations off-world, far from the throne he had sold his soul for.

Grayden leaned back and activated the screen in front of him. He loaded the same file he had been listening to for the past few weeks and as the clipped baritone voice came over the chamber speakers, he listened to each word for a hint; something he might have missed.

Regent Shiloh and crew have survived passage through the anomaly. However, the craft is severely damaged and we cannot return. Warning: the anomaly is a one-way conduit that exits into a neighboring galaxy. Verify broadcast protocols and send new ship for component and supply replacement.

Was it possible? Could his brother really have survived? To find out, he ordered a man sent through the anomaly. But even if he succeeded, his signals wouldn't reach Ehrets for almost a decade. Maybe he could send a pulse from the prisM through the anomaly and force it open so he could travel back and forth.

He held the prisM in front of him. He didn't know of any limits to its power; only that it weakened the further it was taken from sources of human life. Indeed, it had been quiet since Grayden established his headquarters in space. But this week, it had begun whispering and glowing, interrupting the little sleep he got.

The sounds of the audio signal were drowned out as the prisM started emitting a loud pulse. The deafening pulse became wails and the wails were of pain.

Then the prisM caught fire.

A lesser man, unfamiliar with the ways of the spirit, would have seen nothing as the eldritch blue flames licked around the corners of the prisM and traveled up Grayden's arm. He stretched his arm out, trying to escape the flames, but they engulfed his body and he collapsed to the floor in searing agony.

When his eyes opened again, the pain from the flames was gone, but he couldn't move. Someone...something was standing behind him; he could sense it urging him to look around.

Graydenwas no longer in space, but he wasn't on Ehrets, either. It was night and he was in what appeared to be an ancient city, though the buildings were an unusual design that he had never seen before.

He stared at the people walking around. They wore separate pieces of clothing for their torso and leggings, very odd. The smoky chariots that ran down the crude street ways reminded him of pre-gravimetric transports.

Then he saw a body.

Upon closer examination, he could tell the man wasn't dead, but was severely injured. Then Grayden recognized his father's helmet and the mantle he coveted lying in the wet streets.

It was his younger brother, long thought dead. Grayden had never held any personal animosity toward Shiloh, but seeing the mantle that should have been his drove a stake of anger through his heart and he levitated closer. He had moved close enough to touch his brother when Grayden found himself being drawn toward a large building.

He tried to resist with all of his strength, but to no avail. He was taken inside to hover in the center of the chamber. A suit of armor was laid on top of what appeared to be a coffin and above the armor was the prisM!

Grayden looked at his hand. The prisM was still there.

His prisM linked with the other prisM and as soon as they occupied the same space, both prisMs dimmed.

Then came the explosion.

A cobalt detonation of the mystical energy of both prisMs flooded the building, battering Grayden into unconsciousness, but even then he couldn't escape the pain that scalded his spiritual body.

The explosion was felt everywhere on Earth at once. The mystical contents of three thousand years' worth of spells spilled into the physical world, branching out into a million forks, drawn to emotion, the ultimate spiritual ground, changing something each time...

A middle aged man, tired of playing catch up with a world that had crushed his dreams a decade earlier, leaned dangerously far out his apartment window. Twenty stories below, humanity moved at a staccato pace, each swallowed up in the selfish concerns of their own small worlds.

Rob Tankersley had long ago stopped fearing death. It wasn't after his wife took his kids and ran away with a man who could "treat them like they deserved", nor after his friends abandoned him by siding with his ex-wife. The final indignity was being fired from his sales job of six years by the man his wife had run off with.

Severed from all human contact, Rob began thinking

about suicide. He leaned further out his window, closing his eyes in disappointment that he couldn't muster a single tear for his own passing when the lightning bolt struck, knocking him back into his apartment. He fell unconscious onto his back, unknowingly ready for the new life he would begin the next day.

Abunai ran as fast as her scarred legs would carry her across the Iowa wheat fields. The pain of tearing the stitches holding her thigh muscles together was unbearable, but she couldn't afford to slow down her friends.

Raised from birth in a secret installation called The Plant, she was one of only twenty children to survive her crop fifteen years earlier. They were taught sciences, mathematics and several languages.

And they were all trained to kill.

They escaped during a fluke lapse in security that left eighteen guards and two of her friends dead. Their fighting trainer had managed to find them after two weeks. Abunai's friends were trapped in the corner of a barn while she was hiding in a stall behind her trainer. The pain of her wounds wouldn't allow her hands to remain steady, so when she pulled the trigger on the pistol she had trained with since a toddler, she missed.

Angry at her own weakness, Abunai grabbed the pistol with both hands. The trainer walked toward her unarmed friends and drew his sword. Abunai screamed at herself. Breathe, she thought, breathe!

Aim.
Fire.
Miss.

Concentrate! Babies trained with pistols! She calmed her breathing and mustered every ounce of concentration she had into one shot.

That's when the strange blue lightning struck and everyone fell to the ground as if their strings had been cut.

The triplets were old enough to regularly accompany their mother to the store, so Darcy, Marcy and Tim Sweeney had grown accustomed to their car seats mounted in the back. Marcy was seated in the middle as always and her attention was on the pacifier that had just fallen out of her mouth. She continued to suck for a moment, but couldn't feel it. She looked at Darcy, who was asleep with her pacifier. Marcy sucked some more, trying to feel the pacifier she was looking at. A small flare of frustration built into her little heart.

Want pacifier. No pacifier.

Suck. Suck. Suck.

Need pacifier!

Marcy's face warped into a frown as she looked at her brother and sister, docile and sucking their pacifiers. Seeing them, Marcy instinctively sucked again.

Need pacifier!

Marcy began to panic. She saw! She needed!

That moment became the most traumatic moment Marcy had yet to experience in her young life: an extended time without that which she desired. The raw emotions that had been building flooded into a crescendo of panic and her mother turned to see why she was crying.

But it was too late. Tears shot from Marcy's little eyes and she screamed as an eerie blue bolt filled the car, momentarily blinding her mother.

Though she couldn't see, her mother somehow managed

to safely pull the car over to the side of the road. Her first thought was of the triplets' safety. But when she looked back, only Marcy remained in her car seat.

Happy and with her pacifier.

Even the supernatural world wasn't spared. One of the oldest beings in existence was caught mid-phase as it roamed freely throughout the suburbs of Peoria, poisoning the dreams of men. From bedroom to bedroom, it corrupted the ethereal reality that played in their owners' minds.

Yeter'el was in a modest two story brick house indulging a small boy with a dream about dragons. Yeter'el was about to give him a nightmare that he would remember the rest of his life when it felt a rumble.

It had seen many storms over many thousands of years in the physical realm, but it had never before seen a storm rolling through the spiritual realm. The logical thing to do was to phase into the physical world to avoid the storm and investigate later. It merely concentrated and its being changed as if stepping through a door, visible to the world of men, but intangible.

A bolt of lightning struck it in mid-phase and Yeter'el couldn't move. Pain arced through its being as it tried to finish phasing. The feeling was so alien that it panicked. Attempting to make its body invulnerable for protection, only the spiritual side responded. The physical side, visible but intangible, failed to change.

The shock to its system was too much and for the first time in its existence, Yeter'el fell unconscious. Its shriek rolled through the neighborhood loud enough to wake everyone in its range. The young boy jumped from his bed to see the Half-Life spasming on his floor. It is a scene he will never, ever forget.

Bolt after bolt struck across the center of America, forever changing the lives of the people it struck. Then the mystical cloud seemed to sense an unusual spiritual ground in the atmosphere and the bolts arced upward.

Mosh finished linking both ships together when a twisted thought occurred to him; he was doing the same exact thing here that he was in the Toad Squad. He squashed the thought. He would never do this again.

He swore it.

Mosh piloted his cargo ship high in the atmosphere ready to link with the Regent's ship. He had just finished programming it to control his cargo and was calibrating the last few connections before arriving to Earth. Mattis would remotely pilot the crafts out to the rendezvous point as well as control the detonation.

Then something caught his attention. It was a sudden and small prick at the edge of his consciousness, normally recognized only while asleep.

A bolt of lightning etched its way from the planet's surface, phasing through the thick protective hull that shielded his ship as if it weren't there. It carried through the floor plating, filling each chamber. Once it washed through his body, the bolt turned back down with an almost conscious hunger, disappearing over the horizon toward Europe.

Mosh was still conscious, but not in control of his body. He struck his head on a panel as he collapsed to the floor. It wasn't enough to knock him unconscious, but it caused a gash and blood started flowing. Try as he might, Mosh couldn't move a muscle, not even his eyes which were still closed from the pain.

"What happened?" Mattis asked.

Mattis turned all of the ship;s scanners toward Mosh's

unmoving body. The sensors were crude, so Mattis had to tweak them, optimizing their code for medical retrieval. The sensors were more powerful than the Regent's ship and, with their new instructions, were able to provide a complete diagnosis.

Mosh was conscious and there appeared to be nothing wrong with him aside from the gash to his head, yet he was not moving.

That's when Mattis synced Mosh's condition with other odd activity occurring on the planet surface. Something was happening on a supernatural level that Mattis could not detect, could not diagnose and could not assist.

Mattis was helpless.

A spiritual storm raged invisibly above Joliet, Illinois, spitting arcs of mystical lightning across the skies. Inside the warehouse, the sorcerers who had stood around the armor during the incantation lay smoldering in the wake of the eldritch explosion, their spirits battered from their now-empty flesh husks. Even Andris, who was standing a safe distance away, was stunned by the blast.

The only man with the power to leave was Meonemin and as he retrieved his cane, he looked back with a tinge of excitement at the movement on the crude altar.

The era of the Tri-fesT had dawned!

Three separate parts; spiritual, physical and mechanical, had fused into one sentient being. The binary at first refused to accept the input, but the spiritual encompassed the three, intricately binding them into a single impossible entity. Where once existed a technical suit of battle armor and the separate beings of Leif Laima and the arch-demon Argus, now only the supernatural beast USCHI remained.

It thrashed around in newborn exuberance. Seeing the twisted bodies of the wizards lying around only excited it. USCHI tore into the corpses, engorging itself on the organs of the dead with glee. Then its sensors detected a man who lay unconscious in the corner.

Life still pulsed in the veins of this one.

USCHI charged the length of the room in a single angry leap to confront the man, this puny thing, its mortal enemy, to disembowel him and skin him as a trophy before a worldwide purge of blood and entrails. USCHI picked the man up, ready to sink its steely nailed fingers into his chest when something odd happened.

It set the man down carefully, almost tenderly.

USCHI looked at the man, confused. It felt the hunger and rage to pounce rise within its chest, but then stepped back. At each violent thought, USCHI felt something pull it back into a non-threatening stance. Frustration twisting quickly into rage, USCHI roared impotently at the man and launched into the sky to take its anger out on something else.

Anything else.

Everything else.

USCHI leapt across the Cass Street Bridge, landing on the roof of an apartment building. Detecting the life pulses scattered through the structure, USCHI clawed its way down the center of the building, tearing through brick and stone and steel. At the base of the building, USCHI thrashed at the foundation until the building collapsed in a thunder of masonry.

Sensing the dead and dying surrounding it, USCHI's face became a death grin, its bony smile seeming just a bit wider and its eyes appeared to be set just a bit deeper. Building after building fell under the onslaught of USCHI's fury and it hungrily looked for more buildings to take when a sound came wailing out of the rubble and death, freezing its very soul.

A child's cry.

Anya Cardenas had celebrated her fifth birthday party on Saturday. One of her presents was a soft pair of pink pajamas given to her by her Aunt Nicole, who had no children of her own. Even though Anya didn't like pajamas with footies, she was still wearing them a week after she had received them for her aunt's sake.

Anya woke up in the middle of the street in a pile of concrete and blood and mud. The ten story building she had called home her entire young life was now just a debris field and her parents and baby brother were nowhere to be found.

Anya stumbled out of the wreckage in shock, blood and dirt staining her torn pajamas. She headed toward the first figure she could see; a man - a large man – wearing a Halloween costume in front of where her building had stood. She ran blindly to him in a desperate plea for help.

That's when USCHI felt it, impaling the very core of its being.

Innocence.

The Innocence of the Garden, the power of man long ago abandoned by mortals, was rushing straight toward USCHI, judgment wailing in its tender cry.

USCHI cowered as Anya approached and when she grabbed its hand, USCHI shrieked and spasmed in pain.

It could not cope with a pureness powerful enough to make angels quake. USCHI's legs were frozen to the ground until it broke its panicked trance and lashed out at the source of its pain. Back and forth, the steely talons on the back of its arms slashed until the sound of innocence was heard no more.

USCHI roared defiantly and headed to the next building to continue the massacre.

It had been more than three years since Lisa Curtis last attended *Our Lady of Sorrows*. The church her husband had been baptized in hadn't changed since she had been there for his funeral late last year. In fact, as she looked around, it really hadn't changed since Father Pulaski married her and Tom nearly a decade earlier.

The thought brought a smile to her face; the two of them stood at the center of the church, exchanging eternal vows of love before the small audience gathered behind them.

While Lisa had been an occasional church goer, Tom was an active member, and every Sunday morning he would be at the first service. He never really nagged Lisa, but he always asked if she would go with him and she would roll over in the bed and tell him next week.

She had attended a few times voluntarily; mainly the Easter and Christmas services, and of course, when their babies were christened. The only other time she went was for Tom's funeral and she felt guilty over not going with him the week before when he asked.

She should have gone.

She should be going now, for her girls, she scolded herself. But even as the self-guilt tormented her, the thought of Tom's casket brought cold chills to the thought. Tom had been robbed from her at the prime of his life. Their daughters would never know their father. He would never be able to walk them down the aisle in the church where they were married. But he wanted them raised in the church and she would honor his wishes.

It would be like he was still raising them.

Lisa genuflected and slid into a pew. Why had she even come? To seek comfort from the coming asteroids? Though she lowered the kneeler, she couldn't bring herself to use it, so she sat back in the pew and just lowered her head. She couldn't think of anything to say. She knew prayer was supposed to be a simple thing, but despair clung to her like a fog and she had a hard time thinking.

She should be praying for something...

The Witness.

An image of the young man who had earlier stood before her came rushing to the front of her mind. He was powerful, but inexperienced. If he survived the asteroids, would he be able to use that power wisely? And though the news hadn't yet reported that the first asteroid had been stopped, she knew that he was surely the only reason the Earth hadn't yet been blasted into the stone age.

But there were more, larger asteroids headed their way. Though she hardly knew him, she couldn't help thinking that this was way out of his league. He was going to need help.

A miracle.

So, for the first time in a long time, Lisa found a reason to pray.

But felt no comfort.

Shiloh's chest still rattled from the impact with the asteroid, but he was coherent enough to launch into the sky. The mystical clouds still hung low to the ground, but the people walking the streets of Joliet didn't seem to notice. A small arc of lightning struck one woman as she walked down the street and while she brushed her shoulder off in subconscious recognition, the woman continued to walk as if nothing could penetrate the depression she clung to like a suit of armor.

Shiloh headed toward the center of the collapsed buildings. It looked like images of the worst earthquakes he had seen. Dust filled the air, so Mattis imposed a three dimensional radar outline of the area below him.

Shiloh looked for signs of life, but found only one. It erupted from the dark center of the devastation: an armored skeletal warrior almost ten feet tall, wearing a red and silver headdress and covered in shredded rags. It carried in its gauntlets the bloodied remains of a fresh meal and though humanoid in appearance, its sharp, precise movements told Shiloh that this being was alien to the world of men.

As he looked upon the creature, Shiloh knew this was why he was Called back. The asteroids momentarily disappeared from his mind as he ramped up his bravery.

"*I am a son of Arter and this is my Goliath,*" he thought and launched toward USCHI.

He rammed USCHI from behind, knocking it back into the building it was hovering above. Shiloh grabbed USCHI by the ankle with both hands. Its barbed armor bit into his skin, but he held on, slamming USCHI into the ground. Again and again, Shiloh pummeled the monster into the mounds of concrete and steel that had once been homes to people.

The rubble exploded with each impact.

USCHI twisted around, tearing out of Shiloh's grasp with ease and its massive armored fingers grabbed the first thing it could reach: Shiloh's mantle. As soon as it did, it howled as if burnt and let go. USCHI stared at its fingers, looking for damage, but as soon as it had let go, the pain stopped.

That's when it turned to face Shiloh and Shiloh gasped.

He could see the creature on many levels, seeing not just the physical form, but the spiritual being as well. What he saw was odd; a man and a monster, each with its back to the other, but where their bodies should have been separate, they blended into each other with mechanical webbing. There were others stuck like fly paper to the monster, small and screaming, writhing in constant pain. The man bound to the back of the monster looked at Shiloh with weary eyes, but Shiloh could feel the rage behind them and understood that the man would gladly kill him.

USCHI broke the trance by snaking a barbed fist into Shiloh's chest, knocking Shiloh out of the air. He landed in a pile of broken plumbing. The explosion of water and soot covered his location enough to catch a breath.

"You are holding back, Regent," Mattis scolded. "This entity is clearly not human. You can destroy it."

Mattis was right. Shiloh had been holding back for some reason. His newly found temper flared and angry at himself more than anything else, Shiloh picked himself up and launched into USCHI with all the speed he could muster.

He was transonic when he struck and pushed USCHI

back, though it remained hovering in the sky. Shiloh pounded USCHI with everything he had. Fast and furious, the untrained punches were just enough to keep it off balance. USCHI struck back several times, swinging its tree trunk sized arm. Shiloh managed to dodge the fist, but one of the barbed talons on its elbow ripped through his shirt and into his left arm. The large barb punctured the skin, and embedded deep into his bicep. USCHI yanked its arm back and the muscle shredded.

All feeling in Shiloh's arm disappeared and it fell limply to his side. Using his ability to fly as a lever, Shiloh turned and kicked USCHI full force in the chest, but it did no good. USCHI lumbered over Shiloh, punching and tearing into him, mindful to avoid touching the mantle.

Shiloh noted the change in attack and turned his mantle around so that it covered the front of his body. USCHI backed away, but its eyes seared into Shiloh and he could tell it was trying to think of a way to kill him.

Shiloh wasn't going to give it time.

Holding his left arm even though the blood had already began to clot, he launched. USCHI grabbed a steel beam from the pile behind it and swung it toward Shiloh, but he flipped out of the way of the beam and over USCHI's back, covering its face with his mantle.

USCHI panicked.

The searing pain of the mantle was too much and it began blindly thrashing around. USCHI tried to tear the mantle off, but its hands were seared every time it touched the cloth. Shiloh held on from the back, avoiding USCHI's arms and the dangerous barbs attached at each joint.

Incoherent with pain, USCHI rammed both arms behind it so hard that it dislocated its own shoulders. Both shoulder barbs caught Shiloh in his unprotected back. The barbs sank in deep, puncturing one of his lungs. Shock flooded his body and only then did he notice how quiet everything had become.

The sirens that had constantly painted the Joliet background with their chorusing wails fell silent; the water that spewed from a nearby broken hydrant stopped its impotent hissing.

And though he was in too much pain to move, Shiloh looked around and noticed that everything was frozen in time. A curious mixture of smoke particles and snowflakes hovered so still in front of him that they appeared to be captured in clear amber.

Shiloh realized that he had accidentally triggered Speed and inadvertently laughed at the irony of the situation, releasing his breath and with it, control of Speed.

Time resumed and Shiloh collapsed on USCHI's barbs.

USCHI removed one of the barbs and used the other to bring Shiloh to its front. The mantle fell from its face and USCHI leaned back roaring in victory. Its death grin widened as it studied its still quivering target. The mantle that had caused it such pain was carefully watched so it would not be touched.

USCHI turned Shiloh around to see him face to face, slowly, as if wary of a trick, but the look in its eyes gloated over its easy victory, looking at the broken thing hanging at the end of its arm. It raised its armored fist back and a hundred barbed knives grew from its ebony surface.

Then USCHI's head snapped upward and it looked all around as a voice filled its head.

The voice would not be silenced.

The voice would not be ignored.

The voice would be obeyed.

USCHI roared in fury, but dropped Shiloh.

Shiloh lay motionless, nearly disemboweled on a pile of

jagged masonry. From a distance, it appeared that nothing was moving, but the activity inside Shiloh's helmet was off the chart.

Mattis strained every bit of power from its systems devising plans to save Shiloh, moving system processes from everything else, including solving the asteroid problem. Its top priority, before saving even the Earth, was the immediate survival of the Witness Regent.

Every emergency system in the city of Joliet was now diverted to Shiloh's location. Mattis noted that dozens of people would most likely lose their lives because of its intrusion of the emergency system, but Mattis pushed the emergency systems of every local municipality even further.

It monitored the mobilization as every police car, ambulance, fire truck and national guard vehicle in or close to the city tried to converge on the area where Shiloh lay, but there was too much debris.

Mattis had run out of Earthly options, but still it computed. Every process running through its electronic brain raced for other options. One small process noted that if Mattis were human, it would be experiencing panic right now.

Maria honked at the people driving slowly in front of her. They were driving as if it were any ordinary day. Her car was designed to race, and with the world about to be destroyed by asteroids, she wasn't worried about the speed limit. The reason she wanted a fast car wasn't to show off, though that's what her dad believed when he shelled out fifty-six thousand dollars. Maria just wanted to drive fast, but Champaign's horse and buggy era speed zones prevented anything above thirty-five.

She glanced at her watch. The first asteroid should have hit the east coast ten minutes ago, but apart from the minor quake that she felt, she hadn't noticed anything out of the ordinary.

Shiloh had obviously saved them. Maria turned on her radio to hear what happened. The bouncy tunes of the latest pop tart began flooding her car and though she had never heard the song before, she somehow knew the lyrics. She shrugged until she remembered where she heard the song before. In her nightmares.

That's when deja vu took over.

Everything she looked at triggered the memories deposited in her nightmares over the past month. From the old man wheeling his buggy to his car, to the sign with the burnt out letters, to the car in front of her. Then the other part of her nightmare appeared in her minds' eye: Shiloh, dead at the hands of a monster.

Maria turned the car around and raced toward Shiloh's house. She smacked her steering wheel in impatience as she tried to remember his phone number. Every number she tried was wrong. Think! She urged herself. What was his number? Flustered, she called Kristi in desperation.

"Hello?" Kristi answered cautiously after seeing Maria's number on her caller ID.

"Kristi, I need Shiloh's phone number. He's in trouble!"

Kristi had always prided herself as a good judge of character, which, in this case gave her the conflicting information of not wanting to trust Maria, but she could hear the genuine angst in her voice.

Kristi reluctantly gave her the number. "What's wrong?"

But Maria had already hung up and was punching in Shiloh's number. His father answered on the third ring.

"Hello?"

"Mr. Wagner, it's Maria. I need to talk to Shiloh!"

"He's not here right now, Maria. He's..."

"I know where he is! He told me about the asteroid. Do you have any way to contact him?"

"Maria, we're not comfortable talking with..."

The line died as Maria hung up and within two minutes George Wagner heard a loud screech of tires followed by a rapid knock at the door. As he opened it, Maria barged into the living room.

"I have to talk to Shiloh!"

Shiloh's mother entered the room.

"What's all that noise? Maria? What are you doing here?"

"I'm trying to get your husband to tell me how to get in contact with Shiloh. I need to talk with him and tell him not to go to Joliet!"

Maria's features softened and tears appeared in her eyes.

"He'll die, Mrs. Wagner. Please..."

Lillian guided Maria to the couch.

"Listen, we know that Shiloh told you some of what has happened, but we're not..."

"I know, you're not comfortable talking about it!"

Lillian looked at Maria and then her husband.

"George, call Shiloh. I'll wait here with Maria."

George entered his den and locked the door.

"Now, what's this all about?" Lillian asked.

"I know this sounds crazy, but I've been having nightmares ever since I started hanging around Shiloh. They're bad enough that I have to take medication to go to sleep. Today, they made sense. Shiloh is going to get in a fight with...some kind of monster and it will kill him. I have to warn him not to go to Joliet."

"Joliet? Why would he go to Joliet?"

"I don't know! All I know is that in my dream he does and that's where he dies!"

Inside his den, George Wagner spoke a single word into his cellphone: "Mattis." He was instantly connected to Mattis and in the background, heard what sounded like an earthquake.

"Mr. Wagner, Shiloh has been critically injured."

"Did he stop the asteroid?"

"Yes, but as we were preparing for the second strike, Shiloh was Called to Joliet, Illinois."

A chill ran down George Wagner's spine.

"Called? Joliet? What's he doing in Joliet?"

"Once we arrived, we witnessed the destruction of many buildings and..."

"What about Shiloh?"

"He encountered a meta-class tanniyn and was struck down. I have contacted emergency services, but downtown Joliet has been destroyed."

"We're on our way," George said, hanging up.

George ran back in the living room, glaring at Maria.

"Mattis said Shiloh is down after getting into a fight in Joliet. Get in the car."

"Take mine; it's faster," Maria said, tossing her keys.

The unlikely trio hopped in the car. Maria took the backseat, leaning between the front two seats. George cranked the car and took off down the street.

"What happened?" Lillian asked.

"Mattis called it a tanyon, whatever that is."

"I've seen it in my dreams," Maria said, lowering her face. "It's a monster; big and metal, with a skull for a face."

George turned his head away, but Maria still noticed the tear coming down his face.

"How long have you guys known?" she asked.

"Since the wreck," Lillian said. "We almost lost him."

"Have you heard from him since he left?"

"No. And the last meteor he stopped nearly killed him. This asteroid was so much larger. Maria, you must understand how important it is to keep this quiet."

"I swear, I won't say a word."

George picked up his cellphone.

"Mattis. We'll be there in ninety minutes."

"He will not survive ninety minutes," Mattis replied.

George slammed the steering wheel.

"There's got to be something we can do!" he said.

"Emergency personnel are being blocked by collapsed buildings," Mattis replied. "And local helicopter personnel have failed to survive accessing the destruction zone."

"What's wrong?" Maria asked.

George stomped the accelerator, holding back tears.

"We're not going to make it," he whispered.

Downtown Joliet was a wasteland. The wreckage from USCHI's rampage was still hot and vapors from collapsed gas mains wafted through the streets. Apartment buildings had been reduced to piles of rubble as far as the eye could see. The few survivors abandoned their houses and vehicles, seeking any way out of the devastation.

At first they grabbed things that seemed important, but quickly dropped them as they realized the severity of the situation. Several families even grouped together to find a safe way out, helping each other over obstacles.

An elderly man avoided the groups, giving each a different excuse as to why he was walking directly back toward the source of danger. Now he just had to avoid the other looters.

It was eerily silent except for the distant sound of multiple sirens hovering uselessly outside ground zero. The looter arched his back to grab a lungful of clean air. He doubled over, coughing up thick amounts of mucous. If he were younger, he would have been able to nimbly mount the wreckage, but thanks to a bum knee, he had to pace himself. After reaching the top of the pile, he looked around, trying to find something of value. Something was reflecting in the pile south of him.

The pile was quite a bit smaller, but the broken masonry made it more dangerous. As he mounted a dented refrigerator, he saw that the reflection was near a white cloth fluttering in the bitter breeze. He pulled the cloth to get to the reflecting dome and found it was attached to a body. The looter instantly recognized the man who the papers had labeled the Windy City Angel. He reached down to take a closer look.

Blood was everywhere.

The looter crossed himself and reached for the shiny helmet. This poor guy didn't need it anymore and besides, the looter was sure he could get a good price for it. He reached both hands around Shiloh's head and pulled, but the helmet wouldn't budge. He sat down next to Shiloh to get better leverage and tried again, but with no success.

Not willing to give up what he saw to be a goldmine, the looter grabbed a nearby broken two by four and actually felt a shred of pity as he attempted to separate Shiloh's head from his body. He pushed against the makeshift lever with all the strength he could muster, but nothing happened.

Then he had an idea.

He moved the two by four below Shiloh and rolled the body to the ground. The man staggered to the ground after it.

That's when he saw movement.

The guy with the helmet was bloodied but still moving. The looter let slip a curse. What if he saw what he had tried to do and got better? This was the guy the President was talking about! Secret service would no doubt pay a fortune to the guy who saved him!

Reaching into his jacket, he pulled out a couple of handkerchiefs and put them over the gaping stomach wound. Then he grabbed the helmeted man by the foot and dragged his body away.

Away from the intrusive sounds of the emergency vehicles, to his own direction and for his own purposes.

EPILOGUE

The largest of the prisM's eldritch bolts raced toward the atmosphere, leaving a trail of arcane ozone in its wake. After passing through Mosh's vessel, it was stopped by the spiritual boundary around the Earth. The bolt arced back down, over the horizon toward Europe. In the blink of an eye, the bolt veered slightly south, drawn to a spiritual ground.

It struck a mountain.

A thin rock veneer shattered beneath the force of the bolt, exposing the corner of a crystal spire. The spire glowed with ambient spiritual energy as the bolt finished its transfer and then faded as the energy traveled downward inside the mountain.

The few birds flying around abandoned their nests, sensing something very wrong. As if awaiting the birds' departure, the mountain began quaking. Furiously shaking the ground for miles around, the top of the mountain came down in a roar of rock and dust, exposing a palace to the inhabitants of the Earth for the first time in over two thousand years.

The beings inside stirred.

The jealous gods of Mount Olympus stood to their feet, ready once again to rule the world of man.

You are cordially invited to
the wedding event of the year.

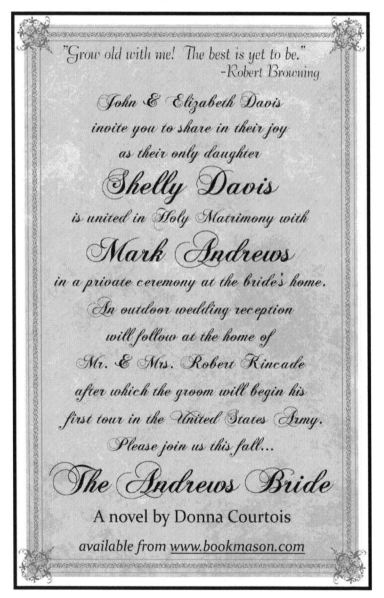

"Grow old with me! The best is yet to be."
-Robert Browning

John & Elizabeth Davis
invite you to share in their joy
as their only daughter

Shelly Davis

is united in Holy Matrimony with

Mark Andrews

in a private ceremony at the bride's home.
An outdoor wedding reception
will follow at the home of
Mr. & Mrs. Robert Kincade
after which the groom will begin his
first tour in the United States Army.
Please join us this fall...

The Andrews Bride

A novel by Donna Courtois

available from www.bookmason.com

MEET THE AUTHOR

Gerald Welch is a husband, father of three sons, writer and graphic artist. He lives in Texas and is one of only four people on Earth to ever be granted the title "Honorary Master of Sinanju".

(If you don't know what that means, I wasn't talking to you)

His website is www.jerrywelch.com where he's always blogging about something or other.

Catch his tweets! http://twitter.com/thelastwitness

THE PROTEAN EXPLOSION NOVELTRACK™

I listen to music while I write. These are the songs I listened to while writing The Protean Explosion:

CAEDMON'S CALL: Thankful
DANNY ELFMAN: Birth of a Penguin
DC TALK: Dive, Red Letters
EVANESCENCE: Good Enough
JEFF BUCKLEY: New Year's Prayer
JOHN LENNON: Mind Games
KARI JOBE: Revelation Song
KISS: Within, Childhood's End
LEELAND: The Sound of Melodies, Tears of the Saints, Yes You Have
MICHAEL W. SMITH: All I Want, Freedom, Missing Person, Eagles Fly
MUSE: Take a Bow
NIN: The Day The Whole World Went Away, The Beginning is the End
NEIL E. BOYD: Somewhere
PINK FLOYD: High Hopes
PUFF DADDY: Come With Me
RICHARD SMALLWOOD: Holy, Thou Art God
ROB DOUGAN: Chateau, Clubbed to Death
SARAH MCLACHLAN: I will remember you
SHIRLEY MANSON: Samson and Delilah
SM LOCKRIDGE: That's My King
SQUIRE PARSONS: I Stand Amazed, Family Reunion
SARA GROVES: Fly, Stir My Heart, Glory Come Down
SHELIA WALSH: Hope for the Hopeless
STEVE VAI: The Reaper
THE BEATLES: I am the Walrus
THE FRUIT GUYS: Blue
THE KINGSMEN: When Crossing Time Shall Come (great song, Ernie!)
TYLER BATES: Remember Us